FREIGHT, FAMILY, AND FIRE

A UNITED CREATURES UNIVERSE STORY

RANDALL FOX

OAKE FOX PUBLISHING

Paperback ISBN-13: 978-1-971636-01-6

Ebook ISBN-13: 978-1-971636-00-9

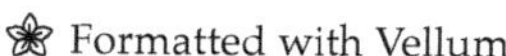 Formatted with Vellum

CONTENT AND TRIGGER WARNINGS

This story mentions miscarriage and child endangerment.

This story contains profanity and weapons, including the use of weapons, terrorism, mentions of gambling, substance use, and references to bodily functions.

The primary protagonist is a child; this story has not been written explicitly for children, but for a general or adult audience.

ARTIFICIAL INTELLIGENCE DISCLAIMER

Grammarly was used to aid with spelling, punctuation, grammar, and word order.

Other than as mentioned above, no generative AI tools were used to create the text of this work of fiction.

CHAPTER 1

CHAPTER 1

My paw hurt. Of course, it hurt; Krissy had bitten it. We'd been playing in the playroom just above the engine deck, like Mommy had said. She liked it when we played. And like always happened, Krissy and Benji wanted to play chase-and-catch, like we weren't sentient foxes. As the youngest, I had to play along. At least until Krissy bit me.

Then I yelped, ran for the ladder, and went up to med. Med wasn't really its own bay, or even a deck. It was a box that sat in the galley. Mommy wasn't there. She was down in engineering, getting ready to shut down the engines along with the crew that had hired on for this run. Daddy was up in the bridge with Uncle Mark, watching as the tail camera, between the engines, showed Marsport growing larger and larger.

I wanted to be up on the bridge. On night watch, Uncle Mark would put the sensor helmet on me. It was too big for my head. I was only eight, and it had to fit him and Daddy, who were full-grown foxes. But it still fit. And it was the best. Instead of being on the ship, it was like being the ship. I could see. The tiny bits that floated in space would make my whiskers—"vibrace" was the big word Mommy wanted us to use, but I still liked whiskers—move letting me know where they were. It even made sounds, not that there were really sounds in space. But it made other information into sound. The only problem was that it stank. It smelled like the stinky cigarettes that Grandpa used to smoke.

A lot of the ship still smelled like it, even though Grandpa had quit going to space before I was born. Daddy said Grandpa smoked that stuff because it helped with how having spent half his life in space made him feel.

I found the med kit. It was kept low so that even I could reach it. I opened it up, pulled out the med spray, and sprayed it on the bite. I wanted to lick the bite. Mommy said I could lick wounds, but only if I couldn't get to the med spray. Licking was good; the med spray was better. But the med spray stung, which licking didn't. At least the med spray tasted terrible, so after I sprayed my paw, I wouldn't want to lick it.

Mommy would want me to go back down to the playroom. But that would mean playing with Benji and Krissy again. I was done with their game of chase-and-catch. I was always the prey when they played with me. I was done with school. I'd done all the work I needed to send back to the school on Earth for the next few weeks, and Mommy hadn't given me anything more.

So I went up one level to my den. My den was tiny, hardly bigger than me. And it was soft, all padded. I'd want to be there when Mommy shut off the engines. I hated zero-g. It made my ears go weird, but being in my den made me feel safe. I'd even added extra blankets before we left Earth this time, so if I bounced off the ceiling, it would be like bouncing off the floor.

Once I was in my den, I pulled my tablet out of its slot and put it into its holder, which also served as a door, making it clear that I was in my den and didn't want to be disturbed, at least not by Benji or Krissy. Mommy or Daddy could come in—or at least stick their heads in, since the den was a bit tight for them to get in with me.

I then tapped the tablet and looked for something to watch. I wanted something fun, but old. Nothing recent, nothing 3D. Old. Pre-

Sentience Wars. Pre-Cataclysm. Human stuff. A lot of folks, both children and grown-ups, didn't understand why I liked old human videos. I couldn't explain it. I just did. Humans, for all their weirdness and all the horrible things they did to bring on the Cataclysm and nearly destroy the Earth, even if that might have been what led to the rise of sentience in every other species, were simple creatures in their way. Easier to understand that foxes, or cats, or Guinea pigs, or ferrets—our crew right now was two Guinea pigs and a ferret, even if one of the Guinea pigs insisted that she was a cavy.

I went to one of my favorites. It was also one of the weirdest, and everyone thought I was strange for liking it. *Star Trek* came out more than 100 years before the Cataclysm, and featured humans and a bunch of other creatures, most of whom looked like humans with makeup, living and working in space. But it was nothing like how anyone lived and worked in space.

I started the video. I made sure I had the version upsampled for species with fast eyes. I once accidentally tried to watch a video, a cartoon about a rabbit and a fox, I think, without doing that, and couldn't figure out what was going on. The images would stay still forever before changing. Mommy explained that humans could be fooled into seeing motion if images changed much less often than foxes do, so we had to make special versions of old human videos.

My video started with a view of the Starship Enterprise, a ship that looked nothing like the Bartlett Family Freighter. Then it moved inside where the crew, all humans, walked around even though the ship wasn't accelerating at all. But this was how humans had envisioned space years before. And I didn't care. My paw still hurt, and we'd be in zero-g soon. So, I just wanted to stay in my den, watching videos and stroking my tail with my paws, until we were docked and, maybe, someone would actually need me to do something—even if I was just an eight-year-old red fox spacer.

———

Jason Bartlett looked across the bridge to his brother, Mark. "510 KM to Marsport dock, confirm?"

"Confirm, Captain."

The red fox nodded and keyed the shipwide. "Prepare for MECO. Prepare for Zero-G."

He then looked at the panel. Engineering went green. galley, all four cargo holds, and the lower berths had been green since Mark had checked them earlier. But the rec deck and upper berth deck both stayed stubbornly red.

"Mark, what is our relative?"

"We're at 600 meters per second."

"We have to cut or we'll start pulling away. We have to check the shipwide. The kits seem to have missed it again."

"Or maybe they just forgot to set the confirms. They are what 8, 10, and 12?"

"Mark, they are spacers. Would we have forgotten anything like that if we heard?"

"Not at twelve—but then by the time I was twelve, both of us were working. Why is Benji still running around on the rec deck like a tiny kit?"

"Engineering MECO on my Mark…. MARK! He's… he has a head for business. He'll do a good job as the ship's master, but he'll need someone to actually fly her. How are things going with that Vixen you've been seeing Earthside?"

"Now, don't you go trying to get me to give you more spacers. You have at least one real spacer in your own brood. Danny is a natural spacer—or at least he's born to wear the helmet."

Jason looked at his brother. "Not for his brother, he isn't. It isn't that they don't get along; I just can't see him working for Benji."

He keyed the shipwide again. "Prepare for flip in 3…2…1…Mark." With a quick jerk of the stick under his right handpaw, the view outside tumbled until the Marsport space station came into view. With a couple more quick taps, the ship was pointed right at it.

"Approach speed check?"

"423 meters per second."

Jason reached down and keyed the comms. "Marsport approach, Bartlett Family on final. Request docking assignment. Transmitting specs and manifest."

———

Halfway through the episode of *Star Trek*, right about the time when things were getting really scary, I heard Daddy say something on the shipwide. But I couldn't hear it clearly. The shipwide was broken on the upper berth deck where my den was. I'd told Daddy and Uncle Mark it didn't work, but they didn't hear me, or they forgot with all the other stuff they did to keep the ship running.

I knew that Daddy was going to tell Mommy to turn off the engines. That meant two things. I needed to get into my den or some other safe place, and I needed to hit the button across the deck to tell Daddy that I was safe. But I couldn't do both. I didn't want to be out of my den when we went to Zero-G. So I stayed put. Daddy would have to know I was smart and in my den.

A few seconds later, I started floating. I didn't like it. I started feeling all sick and upset. My tummy was doing the same flip-flop it always did. Mommy said I'd get used to it. Benji said it was 'cus I wasn't a real spacer. But I knew I was a better spacer than him. He still had trouble with spacer math. He only finished his math for the outbound this time, 'cus I did it for him. He told me that if I didn't do it, he'd take away my blue blankie. I hid my blue blankie in my den, but I still did his math.

I finished my episode of *Star Trek* and then shut off my tablet and put it back in its pocket. I slipped out of my den. The ship was quiet, which meant that we'd docked. If we were still docking, I'd hear the hiss of the jets as Daddy did the tiny adjustments to bring us in. I'd love to do that, but I knew I couldn't. I'd tried on the simulator in the corner of the playroom, on the settings for a kit, and I crashed every time.

Benji watched me that last time, just a few days ago. "Danny, you aren't a spacer. You get sick at zero-g and you crash the sim."

But he crashes the sim, too.

I floated over to the ladder. I looked up—or the direction that would be up if we were moving. Daddy and Uncle Mark were up there talking to someone on the comms. I couldn't go up there yet. I'd be in the way.

Down would take me to the galley, the lower berths, and the play-room. Below that was Engineering, and Mommy said that none of the kits could go there because it was too dangerous.

I just hung there, unsure what I should do. Maybe I should go back and watch more *Star Trek* or a medical show. They were good, too.

"Hey, Danno…" Uncle Mark was coming down from the bridge, muzzle first, wagging his tail like it would help him fly.

I tried to use my tail to help me move once, but I ended up spinning in circles instead, got even more dizzy, and then threw up. That was bad. Mommy had to get the special zero-g sick vacuum and clean it up, then give me the icky space-sick medicine, which made me all sleepy.

"We're almost secure upstairs. You want to come up?"

"Really?"

"Really, kiddo. Once your Dad signs off, the gorillas can start unloading."

"How can a gorilla fit into our ship? It's made for foxes."

"I don't think they are really gorillas… but they are big and strong —well, strong enough to move the shi… stuff we hauled out of Earth's well up here to Mars out of our holds and into the dock transports."

"They'll have to shut the locks between the ship and the holds."

"Yup. I told your dad you're the spacer in the family. Marsport Cargo operations are done in space unless the cargo requires atmosphere handling. And we don't have any on this run."

Dad came down from the bridge using the ladder, but still muzzle first.

He looked at me. "Danny, why didn't you signal that you heard the MECO and that you were safe?"

"I was in my den. If I got out of my den to hit the switch, I wouldn't have been in my den for MECO. And the all-ship doesn't work down here. I barely heard it."

"You were watching human videos in your den, weren't you?"

My ears went flat. "Yes, Daddy."

"And you had your tablet across the front of the den, so all you could really hear was whatever was coming out of the tablet."

"No, Daddy, if the all-ship were working on this deck, I'd have heard it. I have good fox ears, and I don't turn my tablet up loud."

"OK, I'll look at it while we are in port. Now you stay out of trouble."

"I will, Daddy."

Daddy then headed down the ladder towards the galley, where he could check the cargo deck airlocks and monitor the unloading.

"Come on, Danno, let's get you up to the bridge where you can see what's going on outside."

I kicked off the floor where I was and sailed to the ladder. I then redirected myself and flew into the bridge. I kept everything still, afraid that if I moved a limb or tail, I'd tumble and make myself sick. Once in the bridge, I grabbed the edge of Daddy's chair and then pulled myself across to my favorite place, the sensor station.

I slid down into the chair and slipped the harness over my shoulders. I then grabbed the crotch strap. Nobody else bothered, but I felt like without it, I'd fly away, so I clipped it in and pulled all five straps good and tight. Once I was tight in the seat, which was a bit big for me, I felt secure even in zero-g. I then picked up the sensor helmet and slipped it over my head, and turned on the passive array.

The ship disappeared around me. I was the ship. But I wasn't entirely trapped; I could direct how I saw the area around the ship. It was almost like flying. We were alone in this part of the dock, but there was a big passenger liner over on the other side. I focused on it. I could see through the docking tunnels as the creatures transferred from the liner into the passenger areas of Marsport. I watched a family of cats— or maybe they were bobcats, since they were spotted and had short tails—travel down the clear tube. They couldn't be spacers. They were all getting sick, even the grown-ups. It was gross and funny.

I watched that for a while, then went to watch the spinning part of Marsport, but it just made me dizzy.

Finally, I turned to watch for other ships coming in. I could see several, their glowing tails growing larger.

I must have fallen asleep there because I woke up much later, tucked into my den.

———

"Engineering MECO on my Mark."

Regina Bartlett put her paw on the red Main Engine Cut Off lever and looked across at the cavy—not guinea pig—she'd hired as her assistant engineer for this run to Mars. Lauryn Gibbs had turned out to be more than a good engineer and mechanic, but a good ear, even if she was a bit of a snob. Her younger brother Henley was more down to Earth, as the expression went, and didn't object to the more common term for their species. But the run to Mars was nearing the end, and she didn't know if the Gibbs siblings would sign up for the return trip or not.

"Mark," came the command from Jason on the bridge. Regina pulled the lever, and the superheated helium from the fusion reactor quit flowing. Over less than a second, the ship went from accelerating at a constant thrust of 0.8g or 7.84 meters per second squared to drifting at a constant velocity, which was a number that the bridge cared about, not engineering.

"Fusion reactor output reduced to station keeping," Lauyrn reported. "Excess helium directed through chillers to the maneuvering thrust reserves."

"How are we on hydrogen fuel?"

"30,000 tonnes."

"Crap. We burned too much on the way up. We'll need to pay Martian rates or underthrust on the way back."

Lauryn pulled out her personal tablet and started punching in some numbers. "If you load bulk, not mass, thrust at 75, and hold off launch to narrow the window, you'll be able to get Earthside only three months later."

"Won't work. Danny is too young to be spaceside that long. He needs at least 80 for the thrusts, and we're going to push it as it is. I can't have UC child services ground him. I'd have to leave him with my father, or Jace's father. And neither is a good choice. Jace's dad smokes like a chimney, claims it helps with his Spacers, but it's a..." she stopped and looked around. Even in engineering, where she'd repeatedly told the kits they were not allowed, she stopped herself from using profanity without making sure none of them were within earshot—or at least where she could see them. "…fucking excuse. He loves the image, and he's probably addicted to something in smokes."

She took a breath. "Danny hates how they stink. He doesn't say a word, but the way his muzzle wrinkles whenever Patrick is around… A mother can tell. And my dad is still mad that I didn't go fleet."

Ramon, the ferret who had been with them for four runs doing various maintenance tasks, popped out of one of the tiny crawlspaces that ran throughout the engineering spaces. "You're afraid he'll fill Danny's head with tales of the glory of the fleet. Just let ole' FSC Ramon disuade him of that."

Regina looked at the greasy ferret. "If I recall, you got a less-than-honorable discharge—something to do with gambling, or the admiral's daughter, depending on how drunk you are and which bar it is."

"And you got a fleet-trained mechanic who has put this bucket of bolts into better working order than it has been in years, all for the bargain rate of whatever you've been paying me."

She smiled at Ramon. "You are worth at least twice whatever we're paying you, just for the work you've done down here on the engines and reactors. They are purring better than they have since I came aboard."

Henley came up from the reactor control station in lower engineering. "The boards show we're docked, cargo locks are sealed, and hatches are ready for opening. Do I need to go forward… up and help with cargo operations?"

Regina looked at the younger guinea pig. "Go up and see if Jace needs you. He might be fine monitoring both port and starboard unloading, or he might want you to watch one side. Marsport cargo is usually pretty good, not like any of the Earth stations, or, heaven forbid, half the belt ports."

Lauryn looked at her. "I hear that the conglomerates are trying to price out independents on the Earth-Mars and Luna-Mars runs. You might soon have to shift to belt runs or subcontract to them."

Regina sighed. "Post-scarcity economy. Money doesn't matter. Yeah, unless you want to do something other than grow flowers in your back garden. About the only things that I don't need money for are food and clothing. If I want fuel for this ship, I either have to buy it or wait for my allotment. Same thing for parts. And what do we haul? Half of what we haul is stuff that can't be synthesized, which is a lot."

Lauryn looked at her. "We've had this discussion what, two dozen times on the way up, and we'll have it another two dozen times on the way down. Don't you have kits to check on, and probably feed?"

Regina looked at her watch. "You are right."

She unbuckled from her seat, pushed off, and vectored towards the hatch that would lead her to the stairs towards the main decks of the ship.

When she reached the playroom, she found Benji and Krissy still strapped in, working on their homework. "What are you two working on?"

"History—I have a paper on the Pre-Cataclysm environmental and anti-environmental movements," Benji replied. "Remember? You want it finished before we go Marsside so you can transmit it with all of our homework. I still need to find two more citations and work them in."

Regina looked at her older son. He ended up on an advanced track in history and social studies. She would not have ever been assigned a paper like that at 13.

They would have to remember to celebrate his 13th birthday when Marsside, since it had passed midvoyage, and some old spacer superstition said that it was bad luck to celebrate anything midvoyage. She and Jace would also have to fit their 15th wedding anniversary in before returning to Earth, since it would probably happen shortly after departing.

Krissy looked up. "I'm just finishing up that last vocabulary assignment."

Regina looked at her older son. "What about your navigation math?"

"Finished that last week."

"Make sure it is in my inbox. I don't want you posting it directly."

His ears went flat. "OK, Mom." He tapped on his tablet. "I sent it to you."

She pushed and continued up, passing through the lower berths and the galley, and stopped in the upper berths. They were too quiet.

Even if Danny were in his den sleeping or watching one of those old videos, she would hear his breathing. Mark must have taken him up to the bridge again. It was good and bad. He was getting quite the head for sensors, but he needed to work on other systems, too. Sensors were important, but the kit needed to be rounded, not a sensor geek.

She grabbed the rails and pushed up into the bridge, where she found her brother-in-law dozing up against the windows, and Danny strapped tightly into the sensor operator's station, helmet on his head. But his soft snores were audible even through the helmet. Poor kit, he must be more exhausted than he realized.

She pushed off, and with a mother's deft paws, had him unbuckled and out of the helmet in seconds. He massed more than he did a year before, but not so much that Regina couldn't easily tuck him to her body and move through zero-g with him. She quickly targeted the shaft that carried her back down to the upper berth deck, then, with a soft bounce off the floor, she was outside his den. She caught the hand-hold above his den with one paw, and with the other, she reached in and placed her youngest son inside, and then, using her feetpaws to hold her in place, she reached in and tucked the sleeping kit into his den, and quickly placed a kiss on his head, right between his ears.

CHAPTER 2

CHAPTER 2

woke in my den. I'd been in sensors watching the other ships approaching… but I had a bit of a memory of Mommy coming and getting me and tucking me in. Then of Daddy sticking his muzzle in and kissing my footpaw because that was all he could reach.

We were still at zero-g. But after sleeping all night, it didn't bother me as much.

I unwrapped myself from my blue blankie and pushed out of my den. The upper berth deck was quiet. Mommy and Daddy must already be up and down in the galley. But I couldn't go down there yet. I had to do the other thing I HATED about zero-g.

I pushed across the deck and went into the head. I took off all my clothes and tossed them outside, even my underwear. I hung there in midair naked. I really hated this. I stared at the tubes, then at the regular toilet, as if it were at fault. If we were under thrust, I could just pee into it like normal. But at zero-g, I had to find the right attachment for my… my tiny… and then put it on the correct hose and hook it up. And if I did it wrong, it hurt.

I crossed my legs and wiggled until I got over to the cabinet and found the attachments. I needed to hurry, or I was going to be using the hose to clean bits of pee out of the air, and I'd be stuck in here for hours—that had happened before.

I found the attachment that looked like it was my size. I hooked it to the hose and slipped it on. It was just in time. Relief filled me… until I realized I'd need to use the other system as well. I thought of a dirty word, one that I think also meant what I had to do.

I fumbled through the cabinet, found what I needed, hooked that equipment up, and took care of that business.

Then I had to clean everything up, including hooking up all the hoses for cleaning. Everything went down to engineering waste processing, which was somehow hooked to the synthesizer in the galley, which Benji told me just after we left Earth.

I didn't want to eat anything for three days before Mommy explained how all the waste is broken down into tiny pieces, called organic molecules, and then reassembled into our food and all the other things that the synthesizer can make.

Before leaving, I dug into the bottommost cabinet for the thing that Mommy hated more than me. She said I was a big kit, and should use the zero-g toilet since I knew how. But I told her I hated it so much that I'd rather still wear a diaper when we were in zero-g. She still bought me zero-g diapers and put them in the head. I pulled out a clean zero-g diaper and slipped it on.

I then pushed back out and grabbed my clothing, which was floating around the deck. I flew over to my den and pulled out clean clothes: a t-shirt with an ancient Star Wars logo and a clean jumpsuit. I slipped them on and then headed towards the ladder.

Everyone else was down in the galley. Mommy was cutting up the loaf of bread she had baked yesterday. She can't bake at zero-g, so she always bakes an extra loaf the day before we dock, and the day before we flip mid-journey.

"Mommy, I want my bread toasted with Jelly."

"Ok, Danny. How did you sleep?"

"Good. My tummy is settled as long as I don't do too much in zero-g."

"You'll never be a true space fox if you can't handle zero-g," Benji taunted.

Mark looked at him. "Your father had a sensitive stomach until he was older than you. Your brother has more spacer in him than you do."

My tail started wagging, at least until it started making me spin. I quickly grabbed my chair and pushed into it. I hooked my feetpaws around the bottom rail and wrapped my tail around a chair leg for good measure.

Mommy handed me two pieces of toast with butter and jelly. I knew that the butter had come from the synthesizer, and that the jelly probably had too. Almost everything that was used to make the bread —except for the stuff that came from the jar of sourdough mother that sat in the cabinet above the oven, and the water—had come from it as well. I still didn't like to think about that. But it was the only way we could eat in space.

"Danny, did you help your brother with his homework?" Mommy asked.

"He told me he'd hide my blankie if I didn't."

"Tattletale."

"Benjamin Bartlett, why didn't you do your own Navigation Math?" Daddy yelled at Benji.

"Dad… I have trouble with that kind of math. It doesn't make sense to me. Algebra, fine. But the calculations for orbits… they slide around in my brain. Danno just gets it."

Mark laughed. "Natural born spacer."

"You need to redo all of that homework before we go Marsside, well before you go Marsside. You can stay here on the ship with Ramon if you have to."

"Dad!"

"Don't Dad me. Having your brother do your homework is cheating, and we do not cheat in this family."

I almost came out of my chair because my tail started wagging.

———

Jason looked up from the report transmitted from Marsport to see Regina looking across the console at him.

"How bad is it?"

"We made more than we expected… but not much. The early delivery bonus on the titanium helped. The conglomerates are too slow for some of the small builders who like to run on low inventory to minimize storage."

He pulled the shoulder straps to tighten himself into his seat. "But, I suspect you are going to tell us we burned too much fuel outbound."

"We're under 30,000 tonnes. We'll never make it back in time unless we buy at least 10,000 tonnes here."

"At Mars rates, that will eat at least half of that bonus. And Dad needs surgery. Those cigarettes he smokes to make his spacer's symptoms less, are killing him in other ways. If I could find the mongoose who told him that those fu… damned things would help, I'd bite his head off. And then maybe I'd use my words to do it figuratively."

"Jace, you might be one of the best cargo pilots working the runs. But there is something you are even better at: making deals to haul cargo. Once you and your brother get Marsside, you'll do your thing and melt into the colonies, and in a week, you'll come back with contracts to fill our holds."

"And you'll be stuck dealing with three kits, and possibly two guinea pigs."

"No, two cavies, or a cavy and a guinea pig. If you call Lauryn a guinea pig, you'll get a one-hour lecture on how she's a rodent, not a pig."

Regina pulled herself into the other chair and then slid one shoulder strap over her arm to hold her in place. "Are we really going to hold Benji on the ship until he finishes his Nav Math?"

"No, he can finish it on Marsport. We won't get a shuttle Marsside for at least two days, but we have to get Danny out of zero-g before he starts stinking. One of these days, that kit is going to have to get confident with the zero-g toilet."

Regina laughed. "I'd go the diaper route myself if it wasn't more work to clean myself afterward. At least you can use a frontal attachment half the time."

"You've never been stuck on a ship when everything goes out. One time when I was a kit, this old rustbucket had a fusion system failure right after flip. We were without anything but battery for two days. Mark, Dad, and I were reduced to peeing in bags until that old goat, Montgomery, who lived in engineering, got the reactor back online."

"I'll give Benji the good news that he can at least get off the ship, but he'll be stuck doing his homework while the rest of us get to enjoy the wonders of the Marsport habitat ring. And then I'll get the kits and the crew packing for our time on Mars."

"I'll signal Marsport and have them send us a shuttle. So, the whole crew is going back down with us?"

"Looks like it. I think we're stuck with Ramon until… I think we're stuck with Ramon."

"Good, he's the best mechanic I've ever had. Tell him to give the all-ship and the rest of the in-ship comms the thrice-over while we are off. Danny says that the all-ship is out on upper berthing. And it might be out on the rec deck, too. And we should have him rig safety confirms into all of the berths and dens."

"Sounds good. Just don't be surprised if he completely rewires the whole comm system so it works better than it has since your grandfather bought this ship, but in a way it will take you two trips to figure out."

Jason laughed as he turned to the comms to contact Marsport.

Mommy hung outside my den, upside down.

"Danny, pack your small bag. Ground clothes—that means you need slippers and underwear."

"Mom, I know what to pack to go down to Mars."

"Last transit, only two months ago, you forgot slippers, and I had to carry you every time we were outside."

"Nothing on Mars is outside. It's all domes."

"If it is just under a dome but not in a building, it is outside. And outside is raw regolith, and that isn't good for the footpaws of fox kits, so you need slippers."

I pushed my muzzle out of the den and lay on my back so she wasn't upside down anymore. "I hate wearing slippers almost as much as I hate the zero-g toilet." I came very close to saying a word that Benji taught me, but I knew if I said it to Mommy, even about the toilet, she'd take away my tablet except for homework, until we got back to Earth, or something worse. She'd do something equally bad to Benji, and maybe to Ramon, who I think told him the word, too. But that wouldn't make it better.

"Danny, pack your slippers. I'm going to be wearing my slippers, and I don't wear slippers in engineering, OK."

"OK, Mommy."

Once Mommy was gone, I slipped out of my den and pulled out my bag. We did the laundry just before we got to Mars, so everything was clean, except for what I wore the day before. So I had plenty of clean t-shirts. I packed five of my favorites, rolled them tightly, and put them into the bag. Landside meant that I had to wear pants, not jumpsuits. So, I opened that drawer. I hoped they still fit. My jumpsuits were getting short. They never seemed to get tight, but they were short in the legs and in the arms. And it was more noticeable with pants. I hadn't worn any of these since we were on Mars the last time, two months before.

We didn't go Earthside when we were there. It was too much work to go Earthside, so we stayed on the station. But on Mars, we almost always went Marsside. Marsport didn't like folks to stay there long, no more than a night each way.

I grabbed three pairs of pants and rolled them up, and put them in the bag. Then my slippers. I put them on. They made my footpaws feel trapped. And I'd need Mommy to trim my claws. But she could do that once we were in Marsport, not in zero-g.

I then grabbed about ten pairs of underwear and stuffed them in. I also grabbed three of the zero-g diapers, just in case.

There was still room for important things. I grabbed my blue blankie and my tablet. There was still a bit more room. I debated. I could put in another pair of pants, a couple more shirts, or the special pillow I liked to curl up with. After a few seconds of debate, the pillow went in.

I then draped the bag over my shoulder and pushed off toward the ladder. I went down to the rec deck carefully. My tummy was still mostly OK with zero-g. But I didn't want to get it upset before the shuttle got there. Shuttles were worse than zero-g.

Benji and Krissy were waiting there, along with the two cavies Mom had hired to help with engineering.

Mommy came up from Engineering with Ramon following. I liked Ramon; he knew things about our ship that even Daddy didn't.

"Ramon, don't sell the ship while we are gone. And make sure the all-ship is working."

"Yes, Ms Bartlett. And I'll make sure that all parts of the ship can signal safe for operations, not just one spot per deck, like you asked. If I need wire, I'll just have the port deliver it from stores."

Daddy's voice came over the all-ship. "Shuttle arriving in two minutes."

Just a bit afterward, Uncle Mark came down the ladder, muzzle first, using his tail to propel himself. I still wondered how he did that without spinning around. I knew if I started wiggling my tail, I'd end up spinning and make myself sick. Maybe I could get him to teach me once I was no longer so bothered by zero-g.

Daddy followed Uncle Mark by just a few seconds.

It must have been two minutes, but it felt like less when the light on our docking airlock blinked green. Daddy floated over and pressed the button. The door slid open, and Daddy floated in.

We all followed, except for Ramon. When the door to the rec deck shut, the door on the other side opened. We then floated down the short tube to the Marsport shuttle. A squirrel in a Marsport shuttle attendant's uniform directed us to our seats and helped us strap in— not like we hadn't all strapped into simple harnesses several times.

Then the shuttle headed off to Marsport.

Shuttles always moved, a lot. They were so small that every time a jet fired, it made the whole ship jerk. And they had to get spinning to match the part of the habitat ring where they docked, which was weird. Why didn't they dock on the still part of the ring like the big liners?

My tummy was unhappy by the time we got to the habitat ring.

And getting down the spinning part of the ring until where it was, almost, like being on Mars, made my stomach feel worse. I had to grab one of the bags along the wall and throw up into it. I hadn't done that the last time I came down to Mars two months earlier.

Mommy picked me up and carried me the rest of the way to our room, which embarrassed me a bit. But I was also happy. I didn't feel good, and I was happy not to have to walk.

———

Ramon woke from a dream—more of a nightmare. The same one as usual. The one that came from having been on the UC Cutter Nightingale when it tracked responded to the pirates that jumped a small family freighter during flip. It was a freighter, not too different from Bartlett Family. Jason and Regnia didn't know that he had loaded guns in his berth. He didn't know if they were to shoot pirates or to prevent the crew, especially the three kits, from suffering what the pirates might do to them. He was maintenance crew, but he'd been pulled in to help with the aftermath—the freighter had to be put back into operation so it could be flown somewhere for salvage.

He floated out of his berth and directed his long body into the galley. There, he stuck one of the zero-g mugs into the synthesizer and programmed it to generate a mug of black coffee. He'd program it for some breakfast later, probably just zero-g protein sludge. He was long past caring about what food tasted like. He needed energy and nutrition, not flavor.

Once the mug was full, he pulled it from the synthesizer and headed forward, up, as the Bartletts called it, into the bridge. He needed to get on the internal comms wiring to see if he could fix the problems before they got back from their Marsside layover. He'd have seven or eight days. Plenty of time.

As he dove into the wiring, his paws working almost automatically, his mind drifted back to how he found himself out of the fleet. It wasn't from the trauma of the pirate attack, or any of the dozen or so other times Nightingale went into combat against pirates, smugglers, or the others that most of the citizens of the Solar System liked to pretend didn't exist. Most of those he'd processed, at least partially, thanks to UC Fleet Medical's excellent psychology department.

No, it was what happened shortly after that. Nightingale had continued on. It ended up in the Belt, where it ended up at Vesta. He took some leave at Vesta Station. Vesta Station offers three forms of distraction: drinking, gambling, and whoring. Ramon drank a little back then when he was UC Chief Ramon DeSantos. Whoring was out of the question. He was willing to spend time with a willing ferret, male or female. But he had to really know and like them before he'd let them in his bed.

But gambling was different. Not only was it fun, but he was good at it. Card games, especially. Counting cards at blackjack was a good way to make some coin. But if you could track what was going on at the poker table and track the odds without getting caught up in the emotions, that was where you could really make the money.

Oh, money wasn't supposed to matter anymore. Nobody needed money to live. Food, clothing, and even basic housing were freely available to everyone in the UC, and more if you were a fleeter. But if you wanted something special, money was the ticket. And, for Ramon, money was the scorecard when gambling. He had plenty that just sat there in his accounts as a sign of how smart he was—something he was nearly as proud of as his fleet commendations as a top mechanic.

But that night in the casino on Vesta was different. He'd been doing well at the table until the wolf sat down. This wolf, a one-eyed monster, stood well over two meters and massed at least 75 kilos. He sat down across from him, driving the other players from the table.

A young bobcat cub, maybe fifteen, hung on his arm. Ramon's sense of smell wasn't great, having spent the last fifteen years crawling around the tiny maintenance shafts of UC ships, called Jefferies Tubes after one of the old pre-cataclysm video series that young Danny loved, had left his sense of smell muted even for a predator species. But the scent he was getting from her was more fear than adoration.

The game went on for hours, the stakes getting higher and higher. Finally, after midnight, Ramon started making risky bets. He bet his pocket watch, a pre-cataclysm antique, against the wolf's antique revolver. There was money in the pot as well. Ramon won that pot, and promptly wondered what he was going to do with an antique revolver.

The bobcat cub kept bringing drinks to both players. He was sticking with coffee, and she wasn't spiking it, which he took as a good sign.

A few hands after the watch and gun bet, she set down his fresh mug and then whispered in his ear, "If you risk something you really can't afford to lose, he'll put me in the pot. He thinks he has a winning hand."

Ramon looked at his hand and what was on the table. He looked at the wolf. Canines can bluff, but not well. The wolf's tail wasn't as still as he thought it was. If he was bluffing, he was very good at it, Ramon thought.

Ramon patted his pockets, trying to think what might be enough to force the wolf to bet the cub. Finally, he pulled a tiny square of plain-looking silicon out and set it on the table on top of the pile of chips. "I raise this."

The wolf smiled. "I'll put Daisy on the pot."

The bobcat cub growled, clearly angered at being bet.

The next card went down. Ramon looked at it and pushed his entire stack of chips forward. "All in."

The wolf pushed his stack forward as well.

The last cards were dealt, and the wolf revealed his hand: "Two Pair Aces over Eights."

"Full house, Kings over Queens."

Ramon grabbed the code chip and the girl's paw and ran for the exit, not bothering with his chips.

Once he returned to the Nightingale, he explained the situation to the security chief, who relayed it to the captain. Things might have gone fine, except the stupid bobcat mentioned that he'd bet a "small black square," against her.

He was too essential to the operations of the Nightingale to be thrown in the brig for the return trip, so he was busted from Chief to Fleeter Second Class and confined to quarters when not on duty. But once they got back to Earth Station, he was thrown in the brig there.

Four days later, his lawyer, a jackal, a full commander in the reserves, informed him that if he'd lost the code chip, he would have been the first fleeter in a generation to face the death penalty. As it was, if he faced a court-martial board, he could easily spend the rest of his life in the disciplinary brig—not the rehabilitationary brig with most fleet criminals, but the disciplinary brig with the hard-cases who can't be rehabilitated, and those who commit infractions like his. But he could plead guilty to a lesser crime and received a less-than-honorable discharge.

"There is one reason you have this option, FSC DeSantos," the lawyer informed him. "The cub you rescued is Daisy Crocker, daughter of Admiral Crocker, head of Fleet Legal."

By the time Ramon had finished remembering his inglorious downfall, he looked around the bridge, realizing that he'd managed to rewire the entire comms suite up there completely. And he was hungry. Time to head down and get some protein paste.

CHAPTER 3

CHAPTER 3

I didn't really like being on the Marsport habitat ring. The rings on the Earth stations were better. They were bigger, so I didn't feel them spinning as much. On Marsport, I could always feel the spinning. I never understood how taller creatures, some as tall as two and a half meters, could stand it when I wasn't even a meter.

But it was much better than zero-g, at least.

My tummy was better by morning. It growled a lot when I woke in the bed in the room in Marsport. I missed my den on the ship, especially since I had to share a bed with Benji, who kicked in his sleep, and snored—he said I snored too, but I bet he snored louder.

I slid out of the bed and into the head—no, it was called a toilet when we were landside, even in habitat rings—grabbing my little bag on the way in. I locked the door and got undressed. I threw my diaper into the trash, which sucked it into the station's recycling system, where it would be torn apart. Mommy had tried to explain it all to me once, but it was complicated. Ramon had shown me the smaller one on our ship when he was fixing it, but it was just a lot of gears and robot parts, then what looked like a lot of jars—not like the one Mommy keeps the sourdough mother in, but metal jars with big tubes on the top and bottom.

Marsports' habitat ring rooms had bathtubs. So I filled the tub with water—only fourhundred millimeters, never any more than that, unless we were on Earth, where we had plenty of water. I then climbed in and wet down all my fur.

I stood and pumped some of the shampoo into my paw and rubbed it all over me, especially down where I'd been wearing a diaper for almost a day. That needed a lot of cleaning since I'd… I really hated using the zero-g toilet, even for number two, as Benji sometimes called it. I had to work to get that out of my fur.

I then sat back down in the water and rinsed off. The water turned all foamy. When I stood up, I wasn't fully rinsed, so I turned on the shower and rinsed again, which added nearly another ten millimeters to the tub, which was a lot more water than I wanted to use. Mommy would be mad that I wasted water. But I needed to be clean. It wasn't my fault that the Marsport shampoo didn't rinse out right.

I shook to get as much water out of my fur, splashing water all over the inside of the tub. I stepped out, grabbed one of the towels, and dried myself off. It took me a long time to get dry enough to start getting dressed. I put on clean underwear and then walked over to the sink, where Mommy had put her brushes. I always borrowed Mommy's brushes, and she didn't mind. First, I used the brush for my body fur, which took a few minutes.

Then I put on my t-shirt, this one featuring a ship that looked a lot like our ship, and my pants. They were too short, stopping way too far up my ankles. But I still had to pull the belt too tight to keep them from slipping down.

Next, I brushed the fur on my head and arms. Finally, I brushed my tail with the special tail brush. I liked brushing my tail. Brushing my tail felt good. Stroking my tail with my paws felt good. It made me relax and not worry when things got all bad, when there was too much going on around me.

I was halfway through brushing my tail when someone started pounding on the door to the toilet. "Danny, I need to pee." Of course, it was Benji. Everyone else would have let me get ready without pounding on the door.

I opened the door and finished brushing my tail out in the room.

After everyone was ready, which took a long time with only one toilet and five of us, we headed to breakfast. We had to take one of the trains that runs along the habitat to get to the restaurant since our room was nearly on the opposite side of the ring. Daddy says that habitat rings can't have more than one or two stories because going up and down changes gravity, and Marsport's ring is too small for more than one level, but long enough for a train to run around it to keep folks from having to walk.

After I finished my bacon and eggs, which were not real bacon and eggs—not that we ever got real bacon and eggs except sometimes when we were Earthside, and it was a very special occasion—I sat looking around. Two tables over was a creature I'd never seen before in real life. I'd seen them lots of times. Hundreds, maybe thousands, of times. But never in real life. But there, two tables over, sitting with a doe deer was an actual human.

I kept looking at him. I'd seen enough videos to be positive that this human wasn't a grown-up. If the old pre-cataclysm videos I'd seen were accurate, he was only about my age, eight or nine. He was dressed similarly to me, a t-shirt with an old cartoon mouse, and tan pants. He had on slippers—no shoes, humans always wore shoes for some reason. They weren't like the shoes that horses and some similar creatures wore nailed to the hooves on their feet. They were more like the slippers I'd have to put on before we actually went down to Mars because of the regolith outside.

I noticed he kept looking at me, too. There weren't many children around right now. I could see one other family at the far end of the restaurant, but they were antelopes, and I think their fawns were teenagers.

Most of the creatures from the liner I'd seen unloading yesterday had already been shuttled to the surface. The human and his deer companion must have come in on the liner, but for some reason hadn't shuttled down yet.

Mommy looked at me. "Danny, you can go over and introduce

yourself. But be polite, and if he doesn't want to talk, don't push it. And don't go asking all about being a human."

"OK, Mommy."

I stood and walked over.

When I got close, the lips on his mouth turned upward in what I realized was a smile.

"Hi, I'm Danny, Danny Bartlett."

"Max, Max Williams. Can I pet you?"

That was a weird request. "OK, I guess. Most folks don't pet strangers."

"I had a pet dog back... back on Earth. But I had to leave her behind."

"You had a pet dog?"

He reached over and started rubbing his hand on my head. It felt good... good enough my tail started wagging without me wanting it to.

"She wasn't sentient. Some folks, mostly humans, still have non-sentient pets. Mommy thought it would..."

He started crying. Not small cries. But really hard tears. "Mommy's dead. A car hit her because the cat driving didn't have it in automatic and was looking at his tablet. Now I have to go live with Daddy on Mars. I don't know Daddy. He and Mommy divorced when I was tiny. And I miss Earth. My friends. My dog."

I reached around and hugged this human I'd only met a few seconds before.

He put his head on my shoulder and kept crying.

I stood there frozen.

After a few minutes, he sat up. "Thank you, Danny. I'm supposed to go to Mars on the afternoon shuttle. Do you want to play? I hear there is a playground near here."

"Let me check with my mommy and daddy."

"OK. Ms Shepherd will let me play, she said, that was where we were going after breakfast. She eats slowly, being a deer."

After Mommy said it was OK, I took Max to the playground next to the restaurant. We spent time on the slides and swings. Swings on a habitat ring are weird, and I couldn't be on them long before my tummy got upset. I didn't want to get sick again, so I ended up sitting on the not-grass instead.

"Max, Mommy said not to ask about being a human."

"It's weird being a human. Lots of folks don't like me 'cus we ruined things. But that was like my great-great-great-great-grandfather's time. Didn't your great-great-great-great-grandfather hunt mice in the woods?"

"Yeah. And I like old human videos, like *Star Trek* and *Star Wars*."

"I like some of them too, but I like the cartoons. I really like the cartoons that featured animals like you, but before you all became smart for real. Sometimes I wish I were an animal, not a human."

We had fun until it was time for me to go back to our room and pack up for the shuttle. But it was weird, too. Max kept petting me. Sometimes he would forget to ask before he did it, which was a bit rude. But it felt good, even if he didn't ask permission.

Mark watched the rest of the family board the shuttle for the descent to Mars's surface. Jason and Regina had reviewed the financial situation with him, so he was already working through his list of contacts in the grey markets Marsside. Jason didn't like working in the gray, but if they were going to make anything on this run before they had to shut down for six months, it was probably going to take skirting the edges a bit. Jason knew his brother; when push came to shove, he could be persuaded.

He followed Danno down the tube and watched as the youngest member of the family settled into his seat. Danny grabbed the crotch strap on the five-point harness, something that almost nobody else bothered with, and clicked it into the buckle before pulling all of the straps. That kit really liked to be secure in his seat.

Jason laughed. There was one other spacer fox he knew that still used the crotch strap when securing himself. He reached down between his legs, grabbed the nylon strap, and clipped it in place. Danny was very much Jason and Regina's son. But he was in so many ways Mark's nephew as well. He could see way more of himself in his younger nephew than in his older.

Benji was just like his dad, except he lacked his dad's pilot instincts. Jason thought he might have inherited his mother's engineering, but he also showed almost no interest in it. The only part of the business that he had real instincts for was business, which was very important. Jason had seen Benji on the simulator; he was a competent pilot—better than Mark, really. But he'd never have the instinctual feel for the stick that his father did.

Krissy, now there was an engineer in the making. She was her mother's daughter, no doubt. At least she would be once she got past this phase where she was somehow both very girly and very much a hyper-fox. What kind of spacer kit wore a dress to transit to the surface? But Krissy had on a dress, a sensible one, Mark had to admit, but it was still a dress, not pants and shirts like the rest of the family was wearing, or a jumpsuit like he'd be wearing if Regina didn't think that those shouldn't be worn landside.

As soon as the shuttle separated from Marsport, he pulled up his tablet and used the shuttle's internal network to connect it to the Mars systems. A few quick taps with his claws, and he had a secure connection to an anonymous server.

MFox925: Looking for cargo action, downwell to Terra.

The shuttle hadn't even started its deorbit burn when he got a ping back.

PCat572: I've got a load of hooch. Can you handle?

MFox925: Stamps?

PCat572: UC, Marsgov, and Earthgov.

MFox572: Good stamps, real stamps, or trouble.

PCat925: Marsgov real. UC and Earthgov are good.

MFox572: Load at Marsport. Good for vacload?

PCat925: Can do. Will increase upfront.

MFox572: Set meet tomorrow 1930 Mars standard?

PCat925: O'Kelly's. Backroom.

MFox572: Will be with captain. Stamps real for captain.

PCat925: Roger. Good to talk, MFox.

Mark closed the connection. One load of Martian liquor would cover a lot of their expenses, as long as he could convince Jason that the UC Fleet and Earth authority tax stamps were legitimate, and that Paul's price was good, even with the extra to pack it for transport up to the ship. But Paul was a good source. He'd brokered for them several times before, and he didn't deal with the real bootleggers.

His tablet pinged. He looked at the message, expecting a confirmation from Paul, but there was a new message. "MFox925, I have an opportunity you can't pass up—sealed crates. 2000 kg, no questions. €50,000, upfront, €70,000 on delivery, €20,000 early delivery bonus. XHum000."

———

All five points. Even on a deorbit shuttle, I always fastened all five points when I buckled in. Benji teased me once, saying that I only fastened the crotch strap because my private parts were in my crotch. But it wasn't that. It was because it felt right. I wanted to be secure and tight in the seat whenever we were in the bumpy part, like during deorbit.

I noticed that Uncle Mark did it too. Maybe he was like me, or maybe he just did it to make me feel good. Mommy and Daddy just fastened the normal four. Benji sometimes tried to get away with just the lap belts, but the shuttle attendants always made him put on the shoulder harnesses.

This was a good landing. Not too bumpy. Mars is never as bumpy as Earth. Mommy says it is because Mars has a thin atmosphere. But I was still stroking my tail most of the way down. It helped me not notice all the bumps.

We landed at the central Mars Dome not long after. We then had to wait in the long line for customs—many more creatures than had come on our shuttle. Two of the special liners that can land without having to stop at Marsport had landed just before us.

When we were in the middle of the line, Mommy looked down and saw my bare footpaws. "Danial Bartlett, why aren't you wearing your slippers?"

"I need my claws trimmed."

"And you didn't ask before we left Marsport?"

"I forgot."

"I should have trimmed them right after you took your bath this morning, then they would have been soft and easy to trim."

She looked at Daddy. "Jace, how quickly is this line moving?"

"It isn't Reggie."

"Sit down, Danny."

"On the floor?"

"On the floor, and then give me your right footpaw."

"OK."

Mommy reached into her pouch and pulled out a claw trimmer, and she started trimming the claws on my right footpaw.

But when she got to my third claw, Benji started walking forward, fast.

"Shit," Mommy said.

"Mommy!" I yelled, "You aren't supposed to say that. Do I get to take away your tablet?"

"No, but get up and follow your brother."

I got up and had to run to catch up with Benji. Once I caught up, I sat down so Mommy could continue to trim my claws. She managed to finish my right footpaw before we had to move again. Then we got my left footpaw trimmed before we had to move again.

"Now, put your slippers on, no more excuses."

"OK, Mommy."

I dug them out of my bag. They had worked their way to the bottom. I nearly dumped my underwear and a diaper out onto the ground before I got the left slipper out. Then I had to hop on one paw while putting my left slipper on when the line moved again.

Finally, we got through customs in no time.

Outside, Daddy got us a taxi, which took us to our hotel—a tall tower that nearly reached the top of the central dome, or at least near the top of the dome, where we were near the edge of it.

As soon as we were settled in our rooms, Uncle Mark and Daddy headed out to get us cargo to take back to Earth.

Mommy plugged her tablet into the Mars network. "I'm using Mars' high-speed to send your homework for this leg to your school.

I'll have your grades and your new assignments in a bit. Then I think the three of you should spend some time on schoolwork before we go out and see what Mars has to offer this week, OK, Kittos?"

Paul Marx was a ligar, a giant cat, the dead-end result of a tiger mother and a lion father. He was a hulking beast that Jason really didn't like dealing with. He was, however, honest in his way. Oh, he'd lie through his teeth about certain things, but he'd never cheat any party he was brokering a deal for.

Jason and Mark walked into the back room at O'Kelly's pub in the Original Dome on Mars. The pub was one of the first buildings built under the low dome. A historical marker said it had originally been a habitat for the larger workers, then a warehouse for parts used in building the second dome—the current Original Dome—over the first, temporary dome. Over the years, it had served a number of other functions, and now it was a bar with a very mixed reputation on the edge of a neighborhood with an equally mixed reputation.

Paul was sitting at his usual table. The ligar was alone. He didn't need security. Nobody would mess with the giant. His paws were nearly as large as either of the foxes—not their paws, their entire bodies. And it was rumored that before he'd become a broker, he'd spent time on the Martian MMA circuit, only to be kicked out after killing too many of his opponents.

"Mark, Jason, can I get you anything? We have some real bacon-wrapped figs today. Well, the figs are real; we've not quite gotten Martian hog farming working. Nobody is quite willing to bring the breeding stock up from Terra. Maybe you two would be willing… No, you aren't equipped for livestock, are you?"

Jason slipped into the booth next to the ligar. "Mark says you have something for us?"

"Straight to business, I like that about the Bartlett boys—100 kilos of Martian Whiskey, all stamped and ready for shipping."

Jason looked at his brother, who nodded. He suspected that at least one of the tax stamps was forged, but he also knew better than to push it. Paul was good enough that if he thought his forger was sloppy, he'd warn them. The profit margin on Martian Whiskey was too good to pass up, even with forged tax stamps. "How much?"

"€10,000, plus another €3000 for the containers, so that you can load at Marsport without having to pay their atmospheric loading fees."

Jason laughed. "Atmospheric is right." Marsport would charge them at least twice as much to bring out the pressurized loading rig for cargo like whisky. "€7,000, plus the 3."

The ligar laughed. "You're killing me, Jason. 9500, I can't go any lower."

After a few more rounds and some of the bacon-wrapped figs, they settled on a fair price.

As they were walking out, a human walked in, bumping into Mark, nearly knocking the much smaller fox to the ground.

As Jason helped his brother up, he looked at him. "What was that about?"

Mark looked at the piece of paper—actual paper—in his paw. "I think someone really wants us to carry some sealed cargo for them."

CHAPTER 4

CHAPTER 4

Benny's was supposed to be a recreation of some old Earth restaurant. It was filled with fake Earth antiques hanging everywhere and had ferns growing in pots all around. I'd seen a few scenes set in similar places in old Earth videos, so maybe they had succeeded.

But it was one of Benji's favorite places to eat on Mars. We were there to celebrate his thirteenth birthday. He'd actually turned thirteen somewhere between Earth and Mars, but spacers don't celebrate anything while en route. Mom calls it a "silly old superstition," but she won't break it any more than anyone else on the ship, not even to give one of us an extra birthday kiss.

We sat at a fox-sized table in the back corner of Benny's with enough ferns around us to make it almost seem like a jungle, if it wasn't for the child's bicycle and what I think was a television hanging over our table.

I looked at the children's menu. It had a lot of the usual choices for canine kits, cubs, and pups. But a few made me wonder. "Mommy, what do they mean by a 'basket of hoppers?'"

"Crickets or grasshoppers, Danny. But they probably aren't fresh. They are better fresh."

The server, a kit fox—not to be confused with a fox kit—with his tan fur and long limbs, but still not quite as tall as me, even though he was probably fully grown, looked at Mommy. "Actually, we get our insects straight from the farms in the ag domes. They are as fresh as anything, and one of the few meats on the menu that isn't synthesized."

Mommy looked at me. "Danny, if you are feeling brave, you can try the hoppers. But if you don't like them…"

Uncle Mark looked at me. "They really have hoppers on the kit's menu? You should try them. I think I might order a plate. Better than a synth burger, which is the other thing I was thinking of."

Benji looked at Mommy. "Can I get a steak?"

"Yes, you can, but only because it is your birthday. We have to pay for steaks."

I turned to Uncle Mark. "Are hoppers really good?"

"I like them. But I used to catch them wild back on Earth. I haven't had Martian hoppers before. But you might have to be fast."

The server looked at us. "We keep them in the fridge so they are slow. We don't want them escaping and getting into the herbivore's meals."

Uncle Mark laughed.

I looked at the server, "I'll take the kit's hoppers. And fries."

When the food came out, I had a basket on my plate next to the fries. Not a basket like I'd have with a burger or chicken, but one turned over. Uncle Mark had a bigger basket on his plate.

I watched him for a second. He lifted his basket with one paw and stuck his other under it and came back with a fat grasshopper. It actually looked good. I'd never seen an insect look tasty before.

I put my left paw on top of my basket. I then put my right paw next to it. Then I lifted it, reached in, grabbed the first hopper I found, and pulled it out. I quickly popped the grasshopper into my mouth before I had a chance to think too hard about it. It was crunchy, and… wonderful. It was almost as good as real bacon or real eggs. Not quite, but almost.

"Danny, quit hitting me with your tail."

"Sorry, Krissy."

I finished my basket of hoppers in like six bites—but only because that was all they gave me. I then devoured my fries. I was still hungry, but we'd soon have cake, since it was Benji's birthday.

Once everyone had eaten, the server brought the cake. The whole place sang their birthday song. I had to put my ears down because nobody was singing it the same way.

I needed to tell Mommy that I didn't want my birthday celebrated at Benny's or anywhere that made the whole restaurant sing.

At least the cake was good.

———

Mark stood at the end of the alley. It was dark—Martian midnight, which for once was also close to the ship's midnight. For a week-long stay on Mars, the family kept to ship time, which was also Earth time back home. Each Martian sol was about 39 minutes longer than an Earth, or ship, day, so the clocks drifted a bit. This stay wasn't too bad. Two months before, the family was hours out of sync with Mars, which made commerce a bit trickier—especially for Regina, who had to do more mundane commerce activities for the family instead of buying or contracting cargo.

Mark hadn't told his brother or sister-in-law that he was heading out for this meeting. It wasn't that he wanted to meet with XHum000. He didn't, but the last message told him that he had to tell this human, or at least this creature pretending to be a human, to fuck off face-to-face.

This part of Mars, an industrial dome nearly 30 klicks from the central dome, reached through the tunnels, was quiet at night. None of the factories and warehouses under it were in operation. The cycle Mark had rented sat behind him. He had a darter on his hip, under the duster he wore more for camouflage than warmth, even though the outer domes tended to hover around zero at night when not occupied.

Jason might know he owned a dart gun, but he was sure that Regina didn't know about it. It wasn't the most lethal weapon kept on the ship. Ramon had a pair of actual slug throwers, loaded with rounds that would punch through most flesh, but not through the hardened outer hull of the ship. And Jason had his own dart gun, which he kept loaded with lethal darts, unlike the sub-lethal ammunition that Mark's darter was currently loaded with.

A flash of light illuminated the alley in front of him, bringing a face into view. It was a pale human face. European, if he remembered his human sub-races correctly. The human used his—no her match to light a cigarette. He hated the things at least as much as Jason. They were killing his father, and they stank. The things had almost died out before the cataclysm, but somehow, after the Sentience Wars, they had come back into fashion with humans and, increasingly, with other creatures as well.

"MFox… Mark Bartlett, so you have finally decided to come and negotiate." Her voice was high and, if Mark was being honest, sultry.

"Why won't you leave me alone?"

"Because you are going to take my cargo to Earth… unless you want to lose something precious to you."

She set a tablet on the ground and kicked it with her foot, sending it sliding to where Mark stood.

He picked it up. On it was an image. As he looked, he realized it was a view of their hotel room, focusing on the bed where Benji and Danny slept.

"You like your nephews, don't you?"

Mark swallowed. "Yes."

"Well, my friends have them under surveillance. In fact, one of my friend's sons just happened to have made the acquaintance of your younger nephew. It wasn't planned, but it works out for us. They have a playdate scheduled for tomorrow, if I understand it. It would be a horrible shame if something happened to those two boys while they were here on Mars. But accident…"

Mark's tail grew large, and his ears went back. "You leave Danny out of this, and his friend."

"Oh, his friend is right in the middle—or his father is. The poor boy… well, he'll probably be involved soon enough. Our terms are simple enough: agree to carry our cargo, and your brother doesn't have to know. We'll give you something else—machine parts—that you can carry with our cargo in the middle, where nobody will look. And you'll get both payments. The whole €140,000 will go to you, and you can transfer your brother's share under whatever excuse you want. And your nephew won't know a thing."

She then dropped the cigarette on the ground and crushed it under her shoe. "Or, you can say 'no' and deal with the consequences after the tragic accident tomorrow."

————

Mommy took me to the big park in the middle of the Central Dome to meet with Max. He'd emailed me almost as soon as we got to Mars, asking if we could have a playdate before I left Mars, and Mommy had arranged it with his daddy.

It was easy to spot Max when we got to the park's playground. He was the only human. His daddy wasn't there. Instead, there was a dog, a sentient dog, standing next to him. She had long grey hair that fell into her eyes.

"Danny, this is Evangeline." It took him a bit to get the long name out. "She's my governess. That is kind of like a nanny or babysitter, but fancier."

He then walked over to me. "She looks like the dog I had back on Earth, which is weird. And she doesn't let me pet her. She says it's wrong to pet sentient people."

"You can pet me if you want," I remembered how good it felt when he petted me.

"No, Evangeline will get mad. She can take away my tablet, and… she can even spank me. Mommy said hitting is wrong, but Daddy and Evangeline hit me. I don't like it here. I want to go home. But Mommy is…"

He was starting to cry again. But he sniffed hard and stopped. "I don't want to cry. Daddy says I have to be a big boy, so I can do big-boy jobs soon. Daddy works with scary folks."

He looked around and pointed to the big slide. "Let's go play on the big slide. We're not in the spinny space, so it should work better."

He ran towards the slide, and I followed him.

We played on the slide, then played hide-and-seek games, which I was better at. I could always find him by his smell, and I could hide in smaller places where he didn't think to look.

The whole time I was with Max, my tummy was doing a weird flippy thing. It wasn't like zero-g. It was like someone was watching me. It was like when Benji was play-hunting but didn't tell me. But I didn't tell Max, because he seemed to be happy to be with me, and he wasn't happy with his Daddy.

Our playdate ended too soon. But it was noon—Mars noon—before I knew it, and that was when Max had to leave. He was going to be going to school, real school, on Mars, and he needed to go there to get started.

So Mommy and I headed back to our hotel. We'd need to leave for Marsport and our ship in another day. And I knew I'd probably never see Max again.

"Mommy, I miss Max. He's sad."

"I know, honey. But some folks get bad luck. His mom died, and he has a bad dad. I'll let the Martian authorities know that he… how things are, and they might be able to help. But that might not be any better."

"I wish he could be part of our family."

"I know, honey. But we're a complete family, OK, kitto."

"OK. I love you, Mommy."

"I love you, too, Danny."

———

Jason looked at his brother across the table in their suite.

"I have to admit it, Mark, you pulled it off again. That machine parts deal will just about fill the holds. And Martian parts are almost as good as orbital parts, and a whole lot cheaper. We'll make a mint selling them back down on Earth."

Mark's tail should have been wagging harder. Mark didn't compliment him enough for his ability to pull off deals. Something was bothering his younger brother.

"What is wrong, Mark?"

"Nothing, Jace. I… ran into an old acquaintance the other day."

"I noticed you snuck out the other night. You took your duster and darter. I worried you were going to make some sort of a deal like you did during those days when it was just the three of us."

"You mean when Dad had stepped down and left a twenty-year-old wet behind the ears kit in charge, along with his seventeen-year-old brother with a chip on his shoulder, and the twenty-two-year-old vixen who was slightly more into the older brother, but was mostly looking to see how mad she could make her UC Fleet Captain father by flying with a pair of spacers instead of enrolling in the academy?"

"Reggie had completed three years at the academy when she met us and decided we had a better way. And she then spent a year in the civil services before she ever took flight with us."

Mark laughed. "But it wasn't until the three of us hit the space lanes without proper supervision that we started really getting into the… bad shi—stuff."

Jason looked down at the tables. "Well, six Martian months in Mars' prison made me decide that it wasn't worth it to carry that shit."

Regina looked over at her husband. "Jace, the kits are just in the next room."

"Sorry… as I was saying, but you never seem to have quite lost the edge. What were you doing the other night?"

Jason looked down. "I had to get some fresh air, well, as fresh as air ever gets anywhere but Earth. So I went for a ride in the tunnels."

"The duster?"

"It's safer to ride with something to protect me in case I take a tumble."

"And the darter that you don't think I know you had with you."

"Not all parts of Mars are safe. And I only have sublethal, unlike someone else I know."

Jason's ears grew warm. His dart gun up on the ship was loaded with darts that could kill any sentient creature, and a lot of non-sentient creatures. But it was a precaution, too many small cargo operators had been jumped over the last few decades, and he wasn't going to let his ship get taken. He figured he could get to any of the hatches and repel any borders—or he could… he could repel any borders. He was always armed during flip and at a few other key times. Reggie knew, and Mark knew. The kits didn't need to know, at least not yet.

"We go back up to Marsport tomorrow. Then the two of us can transit to the ship. Reggie, the kits, and the squeakers can follow in a couple of days."

"Calling guinea pigs squeakers is considered specieist, Jason," Regina reminded him.

"If they didn't squeak when they worked…"

Regina looked at him. "I'll see if I can get us booked at Marsport for two nights. They don't like having anyone there longer than necessary due to capacity constraints. They might only give us one night."

"I know. But we have a lot to load. It could be a three-day load, and Danny…"

"Danny gets better the longer he is in zero-g, you know that. And I will deal with his other issue. He'll outgrow that, too, I did."

Mark laughed. "Yeah, about the time you had Benji."

"Early pregnancy at zero-g was an incentive to learn to use the toilet."

CHAPTER 5

CHAPTER 5

Mommy got us up extra early. We had to catch an early launch back to Marsport. I'd launched so many times it shouldn't be scary, and it wasn't. But it was shaky even from Mars. Sometimes on Earth, we'd get to take the elevator. That was long and slow, then we'd have to take a suborbital from home, which was almost like taking a shuttle, except not as shaky since it never quite left the atmosphere. But Mars didn't have an elevator.

I didn't eat much breakfast, even though Mommy told me a full tummy would be better. A full tummy just meant more to throw up if I got sick from the launch or the docking. Even though zero-g made me feel icky more often, I actually got sick more from launches. And I got sick just after getting to Marsport last week.

Before we got on the launch, which was actually a shuttle turned on its side, Mommy gave me the anti-sickness medicine, which always tasted bad and made me really sleepy. I wasn't sure if being sick was better.

I went down the ladder, which was under the floor when it was a shuttle, until I reached my seat. I then climbed in, fastened all five straps, and pulled them nice and tight until the seat was hugging me, just like I liked. Because the medicine was making me feel sleepy and funny, I pulled my blue blankie out of my bag and tucked it carefully under the straps and even the buckle, and made sure I was holding onto it.

I then fitted the mask over my muzzle. I had my own mask, which Mommy had packed. We all did. For launch, we had to wear masks, even if we didn't for landing.

Mommy said that not too long ago, we'd have had to wear suits for launch. I've only had to put on my suit once. It is the same size as Benji and Krissy's suit, so when I put it on at only five, I could only fit my head in the head part. Everything else was in the chest. But I think now, I might be able to get my arms partly into the arms, but it still wouldn't be like when Mommy, Uncle Mark, or Daddy are in their suits. They can do stuff in their suits. All we can do is not die.

It took forever for everyone to get onto the shuttle. Half the folks were going onto a big passenger liner, and this was a big shuttle. Most of them had no idea what they were doing, so the attendants had to help them with everything, straps, masks, and putting their stuff away. I had to lie there for like an hour, on my back, strapped in nice and cozy, but with a mask breathing the weird-smelling air.

Finally, the pilot came on and announced that we were clear to launch. I squeezed my eyes shut and pushed my ears closed like I always did during launch. Then I got very heavy. Heavier than I was on Earth, almost as heavy as I was during launch from Earth.

When I finally opened my eyes and ears, it was dark outside the tiny window next to Krissy's seat. I could also tell we were in zero-g. I must have fallen asleep, which was good. My tummy wasn't too bad. That was the medicine Mommy had given me.

"We will be docking at Marsport in five minutes," A flight attendant announced. I couldn't see her, but I knew it wasn't the pilot. He'd be too busy to be talking to us if he were about to dock. "We will be docking in the zero-g dock. Liner passengers will disembark first, then transit passengers."

Krissy had taken off her mask. "Great, we'll be stuck even longer. And my tablet is in my bag."

She then looked at me. "Hey, look who is awake. Danny, get your mask off. We're up, and you don't need it anymore."

I fumbled the mask off and handed it across the aisle to Mommy, who put it away in her bag.

———

Regina floated in the hub at Marsport, glaring at the squirrel who looked back with that frustrating expression that customer service creatures somehow all maintained when they were sure that they were right and couldn't solve a problem.

"Right here," she pointed to the email from Marsport lodging. "We got confirmation for two nights of rooms—two rooms, one for two large rodents, and one for four large foxes, three kits, and an adult. See the confirmation code, the digital signature, and everything."

The squirrel, Kinsley, according to her nametag, bushed her tail out. "I don't know what to say, but according to our records, those reservations were canceled… the ones for the foxes. The cavies' reservations are fine. The Gibbs' single is ready for them."

Regina's ears went flat. "The Gibbs are siblings, brother and sister, not a couple. They need a double, not a single."

"We're all filled up tonight. If you were mice, I might be able to squeeze you in, but if you look out there, you'll see the Mars Queen. She just offloaded, and almost everyone is overnighting up here before going Marsside."

"Do you have a record of the cancellation? Shouldn't an email have gone out… or something?"

"Let me check." The squirrel did a quick kick-turn and flew back into an inner office, leaving Regina floating there.

Danny floated up next to her. "Mommy, I need to pee. I didn't think we were going to be in zero-g this long, so I didn't…" He put his paw on her shoulder to pull up to her ear to whisper, "…put on a diaper."

"Can't you use the zero-g toilet here?"

"No, if I have… I can't clean it."

"Benji, take your brother down the spoke into the habitat and find him a restroom, stat."

"Mom, what does stat mean?"

"It means if your brother has an accident, you are the one cleaning him up."

She watched as Benji grabbed Danny by the arm and yanked him into the nearest shaft down towards the habitat ring.

After another eternity, the squirrel returned. "The records show that your reservation was canceled because you used an expired credit account. Did you make sure that you checked the Mars calendar dates on your credit accounts?"

Regina pulled up her credit account information. Her account codes were still valid… but if she put in the Earth dates instead of the Mars dates, and the system processed them without a check… "Fuck…" She quickly looked over to see Krissing hanging just under her elbow, ears flat, having heard exactly what her mother just said.

"I need to arrange for transport to a docked freighter, and I need to send a message to the freighter."

"I can have an in-port shuttle here in three hours. You can head down-spoke to the restaurant and wait, but be back in two and a half. But I'll need an active credit account. And you'll need to grab your boys—they just went down a spoke that is opposite the restaurant.

———

"Danny, did you drown?"

Benji was being his usual impatient self. "I'm… Benji, I had to change."

"Danny, one of these days, I'm going just to grab you and show you how to use the zero-g."

"Benji, it… It hurts me half the time when I use it. I don't like it."

He leaned against the door. "Danno…" Benji never called me "Danno," that was mostly what Uncle Mark called me. But if he was calling me that, he was really trying to be friendly. "It hurts me, too, some of the time. I told Dad once, he said that they make them to work for fully grown, bigger creatures, like horses and elephants, even on a ship like ours, that anything much bigger than a fox can't even get through the hatch."

"But sticking… it in there to pee."

"Danno, just remember to put on your diapers before you might ever have to go into zero-g until you are ready to use the zero-g, OK. And if anyone, I mean anyone, other than me makes fun of you about it, they will be facing the wrath of Benjamin Bartlett, got it."

"Even Krissy?"

"Especially Krissy."

I pulled up my pants and tightened the belt. I then slid back the latch and tried to push the door open. "Benji, I can't get out. You are still leaning on the stall door."

"Oh, sorry, Danny."

We headed out and back into the shopping promenade where we'd ended up after coming out of the spoke from the hub. Benji had pulled me down so hard that we'd crashed into the soft padding they put at the end for grounders who come off the ships. We were both horribly embarrassed, or I would have been if I hadn't been in such a hurry to find the head, toilet.

I looked around. "Benji, where is the shaft?"

"Fuck if I know… heck if I know."

"Benji…"

"If you tell Mom I said that, I'll noogie you for a week. And that will just be the start of the trouble you'll be in."

I started looking around. I then saw the map on a square pillar at the end of the little hallway, where the bathroom was. I walked over to it, but found that up close, all I could easily reach was the listing of shops; the map itself was too high for an eight-year-old red fox "Benji, can you read the map?"

He walked around the pillar and came back. "What kind of idiot puts the only map to the shopping promenade at a level where not everyone can read it. You might be a tiny kit, but you are still taller than most mice and many squirrels. Even I can only really see the bottom half, and the 'You are here' isn't on that part."

He bent over. "Get up on my shoulders, and keep your tail out of my face. You'd better have wiped your butt."

"I only had to number one."

"Still, and no farting."

I managed to get onto Benji's shoulders.

He lifted me, but he grunted the whole time.

"I don't mass that much, and this is Martian gravity."

"You are massive enough, Danno. You've massed up since the last time I picked you up, that is for sure."

"OK, I have it. We need to go past the toy store, which is over…" I spotted the toy store. "…there. Then we just have to turn right, and we'll see it."

He squatted down, and I slid off.

But, since I slid forward, my tail went over his muzzle, and he started sneezing when it hit his nose.

"What have you been dusting your tail with?"

"Nothing."

"Are you sure?"

"Yes… Well, I was in the park the other day."

We started heading towards the toy store when I heard a beeping coming from my bag. "Benji, my tablet is beeping… like I have an important message."

"Who would be sending you an important… wait a second, I'm getting one, too."

He opened his bag and took out his tablet. "Mom wants us to take the train to the restaurant and meet her there."

I looked around. "I don't know where the train is."

"I'm not picking you up to look at the map again."

"Maybe there is a better map by the shaft."

"I hope so."

———

Ramon looked around the bridge. Everything looked shipshape. All the panels were back in place, the wires tucked in. Just an hour before, most of the panels were strapped down in the pilot's seat while he inspected the wiring. What had been a rat's nest—no offense to the many rats he'd known, both growing up in the slums that had risen from the former human city of San Antonio and during his slow rise and rapid fall through the enlisted grades of the United Creatures Fleet

—was now neat bundles of wires and fiber lines organized by function and destination, and labeled for future maintenance.

"System, launch internal communication systems test DeSantos one."

He then launched his sleek body down the ladder, slowly flying down the levels of the ship from the bridge, as pre-cataclysm music blared out of the all-ship speakers: "Is this just real life?"

Ramon paused in the upper berths, where he'd found the speakers both cracked and the wires loose. "Is this just fantasy? Caught in a landslide, no escape from reality." Everything was sounding good.

He pondered the odd lyrics as he continued into the galley. The hard surfaces reflected the human signer's voice oddly as he complained about being a poor boy. But the voice could be heard clearly everywhere.

Lower berthing was good, even in the more private berths that were used by guest crew. Ramon hung outside his own berth. Was he really guest crew at this point? He had no real desire to find another ship as long as the Bartletts would let him stay; he would stay. Even after Jason and Regina decided that they were done with their days in space, and it became Benji's ship, Ramon was willing to remain their maintenance worker.

He knew that day was coming sooner than the family realized. In nine or ten years, Jason would start to feel the effects of his time in space. Ramon knew when this old boat had gotten good shielding. It wasn't more than ten years ago. Before that, everyone on board was getting blasted with radiation. Between the radiation and spending half their year in it, even as a kit, foxes like Jason and Mark would start showing signs of Spacers at a young age.

Ramon had been suffering from his own Spacers for some time. But it hit mustelids differently than canines. He didn't get the shakes. For him, it was more about the loss of senses—his sense of smell was mostly gone, and his hearing wasn't what it once was. But as long as his eyes and paws were good, he could continue to turn a wrench.

And when they weren't… well, there was the airlock. He'd wait until he was left alone on the ship, like he was now. Then he'd pack his belongings into his bag—all except for that shot he'd carried for three years now, the one that the back alley doctor on Luna said would give him about one minute before he'd be so asleep that he wouldn't feel anything. He could program the airlock for an automatic cycle—without proper depressurization—and then give himself the shot. He'd be asleep when he hit vacuum. And for Ramon DeSantos, when the time came, that was how he wanted to go.

But that was the future, and it was twenty or more years off. Until then, he had this family of foxes to serve.

The all-ship was working, so he reversed course back to the bridge. The Bartletts were on their way back. Jason and Mark would arrive within the hour to supervise cargo operations. And the second message from Marsport said that the rest of the family would be only a few hours behind them due to a glitch with Marsport housing. He still had work to do. There were bits of insulation floating around the ship that needed tidying. And he needed to clean his guns before they headed out—and that was something to be done only when he was the only creature on the ship.

CHAPTER 6

We sat in a corner booth of the Marsport Restaurant until we could catch the shuttle to our ship. Mommy was still mad. I could tell. Every time she thought none of us were looking, her ears went down.

I spent that time on my tablet working on my new homework. I had a lot. I was in what the school on Earth called "accelerated maths."

I had to ask Mommy once why they called it "maths," not "math."

She explained that even after the near-complete collapse of human civilization and the rise of sentient creatures, English wasn't really the same language everywhere on Earth. Where we lived, North America, we spoke one kind of English. But our School was halfway around the world in a place called Australia, and they spoke slightly differently, including calling math "maths."

"Davy," she further explained. "You know the Shermans?"

"They are the koalas who also own a cargo ship, but they fly the part of the year when we're stuck on Earth. We see them sometimes when we're heading down and they are heading up."

"They are from Australia."

"They have funny accents. Why don't folks from Mars have a funny accent?"

"The North American accent and the Martian accent sound a lot alike."

I looked at my newest set of maths assignments. It was something interesting called set theory. It wasn't like math, but it was. It was all about grouping things. But I could see how it applied to numbers, even before the teacher in the recorded lecture explained sets of numbers.

"Danny, are you OK?"

I looked up at Mommy. "I'm fine."

"You seemed upset after your playdate."

I stopped the lecture on sets and took my headphones completely off. "I kept thinking someone was watching us. It felt like when Benji or Krissy is playing hunt, but hasn't told me that they are playing."

Benji looked at me. "That is the best way to play. And you do it too, I've seen you."

"I told you, I don't think Max is in a good place. I don't like what you said about his dad hitting him. But there could be more. But there isn't anything we can do."

"I know. He's a nice person, but I only met him twice. It's not like he's a real friend or anything."

"Danny, do you have any friends?"

"Mommy, I spend half my year on the ship."

"Benji has friends. He has to talk to them on his tablet. But folks have been doing that for centuries. I grew up in the fleet. I mostly lived in one or two places, but I had to move to postings sometimes when my father had to... And I had to use email and other things to have friends."

"Mommy, why don't you talk about your dad?"

"My dad and I don't get along. He didn't like that I didn't join the fleet. He's not really a nice fox. He's very strict and... The only creature from the fleet you've ever met is Ramon, and he's not very fleet-like. Not anymore. And that is because he got hurt by the fleet, like I did."

I looked down at my tablet. "You don't like the fleet?"

"No, I just don't really like the way it changes creatures. Maybe it's getting better. But… Or maybe it is just that every time I see a fleet officer, I see my father. I didn't have a daddy or a dad, I had a father."

I looked at her. "Isn't father just a different word for dad?"

"Not to my father."

"Mommy, why are you crying?"

"I'm not crying, Danny. Now go back to your math homework."

"It's maths, remember. Our school is in Australia."

Mommy started laughing.

———

"Jace, the first load of cargo will be the machine parts." Mark looked at his tablet, where he'd received a copy of the loading schedule from the Marsport Cargomaster's office. As the ship's second officer, at least on paper, the cargomaster would send this information to him, and only copy the captain as a courtesy. "I can supervise the loading. I'll let you handle the delicate stuff that comes later."

"You don't trust yourself around €10,000 of whiskey?"

"It will be in vacuum-safe containers until we pressurize the hold. It's not like I could sample even if I wanted to."

"OK, I want to run some systems checks."

"You don't trust Ramon?"

"I trust him completely. I just want to see what improvements he's made. The last time he worked on bridge systems, it took me two days to find where my seat adjustment controls had been moved to."

"Don't forget to purge his diagnostics programs. I don't want to say the wrong thing and suddenly have the bridge filled with ancient human songs."

"I like his taste in music. Although that 'Fox on a Run' that has nothing to do with foxes was a bit weird."

Mark laughed. "I think humans used a lot of animal imagery back in the day."

He then looked at his watch and the Cargomaster's schedule. "If I'm going to supervise the loading, I'll need to suit up. Spacer rule one: don't suit up alone."

Jason laughed. "That is actually about the fifth Spacer rule one. Most of Dad's spacer rules were rule one."

They both vectored down to the galley, then to the back half, where it became the cargo access deck. Mark floated over to the suit lockers and opened his locker. His hardsuit stood there, ready for him to slip into. He turned his back and drifted into it, letting his tail find the tube that held his thick brush. Then he pressed his legs and footpaws into the legs of the suit. Finally, his arms went into the suit's arms.

Before closing the front, he did a quick check. "Right shoulder, elbow, wrist, paw—all fingers. Left shoulder, elbow, wrist, paw—all fingers. Right hip, knee, ankle, footpaw, Left hip, knee, ankle, footpaw. Tail. All good. Ready to close."

Jason drifted over and helped him close the front of the hard suit and check the seals. Then it was the helmet, the tanks, and the dozens of other checks that went into any operations in the depressurized hold, themselves a tiny fraction of what would be needed for an actual EVA.

Mark was glad he hadn't had to do an EVA in two years. Ramon had done two EVAs since he'd come aboard, and Mark had been his suited backup both times, waiting in the airlock holding the ferret's tether and ready to reel him back in if anything happened. But that was the closest he'd come to facing the black than he'd been in a while. The ferret seemed to enjoy facing the black, so Mark was glad to let him do it.

They drifted towards the airlock that connected them to the port side of the cargo deck, which was still depressurized from unloading.

"Lock pressurized," Mark stated.

"Lock Pressure confirmed."

Mark pressed the button to open the lock and stepped inside, then pressed the button to close the door.

"Comms check."

"I can hear you," Jason confirmed.

"Depressurizing now." Mark stood there, feeling the air from the lock pumped into the reserves. Air was too precious to waste any more than necessary, so before any part of the ship was opened to the vacuum of space, as much air as possible was pumped into a reserve.

Once the pressure in the lock and the hold were equal, the outer door was opened, and Mark stepped out. He tied his line to the stanchion right outside the door and headed to the main cargo hold door.

Over the next few hours, the Marsport cargo handlers loaded the crates of Machine parts into the hold. Mark noted that there was nothing suspicious about the cargo. He checked the mass stickers and ensured the loads were balanced correctly. An unbalanced load would make the ship handle poorly. The zero gravity of space meant that cargo had no weight, but it still had mass. And mass meant momentum, and when the ship flipped or performed other maneuvers, that momentum mattered.

Once the cargo was loaded, Mark went back into the airlock, reversing the process until he was out of his suit. By that point, the rest of the family, and even the two cavy guest crew, were back on board.

Once they got the extra 20,000 tonnes of fuel that he'd ordered out of his own accounts, thanks to a mysterious benefactor who had paid back an old loan he'd forgotten about—or so he told Jason and Regina —and the whiskey was loaded early the next morning, they could request clearance from Marsport for departure, and head towards Earth.

———

Departure day. I was in my den, but I'd hooked my tablet up to various cameras around the ship.

Ramon had shown me how to watch what was going on after we got back from Mars.

That evening, I was sitting in the kitchen working on my English homework, reading some really confusing old poem called "The Jabberwocky," when the ferret slid up next to me.

"Danny, I have something to show you. When I was fixing the comms, I put all the ship's cameras online, mostly for you."

He then tapped on the ship system's page and an icon that looked like an old camera symbol—just a square and a triangle. He then showed that it had a bridge, engineering, and various exterior cameras. It also included some sensors that mapped to visual data.

"Now you can see what is going on even from your den, like a real spacer, not like some passenger."

I looked at him. "Will Daddy be mad?"

"No, this is useful for everyone. I'm sure once your dad or mom finds it, they'll start using it too, and just say, 'Ramon did it again.'" He then ruffled the fur on the top of my head and headed back down towards Engineering or his berth.

On the screen, I saw Daddy and Uncle Mark strapped into their chairs on the bridge. I could even tell that Uncle Mark had his crotch strap fastened. Mommy was down in engineering at the main console with the lady guinea pig, who would get mad if you called her that. I could also see that we were still held by the docking clamps.

But then they released, and Daddy tapped the stick, and we started drifting away from our docking position. After a few seconds, Daddy grabbed the stick, and we flipped. I'd never actually seen Daddy flip the ship. It was faster than I realized. And seeing it, even on my tablet, made it not feel so bad in my tummy.

"Ten minutes until we're clear to light the candle."

I didn't understand why Daddy called turning on the main engine "lighting the candle," but he always did.

"Warming up the reactor to full power," Mommy's voice came back over the comms. Mommy's replies had never come through the all-ship before. That must have been another of Ramon's improvements.

I could tell I was going to have to pee soon, but I could hold it for another ten minutes. Then I could pee in the real toilet and change out of the diaper I'd put on that morning. Maybe in the evening, Mommy would let me take a bath. She usually let me take a bath after I'd had to wear a diaper for a day or two, since my fur would stink otherwise.

Benji was right. I needed to learn to deal with the zero-g toilet.

I was tired of schoolwork. I'd done all of my maths. And my English was going to need Mommy's help, but not until she was done with engineering and getting the kitchen set back up for thrust.

I could look at social studies, but that was boring. It was all stuff about the Sentience Wars. That should be exciting, but school made it all about dates and which group of creatures wanted what. It wasn't anything like the wars in videos—except that creatures still got killed, and these were real creatures, including foxes that were related to my grandfathers' grandfathers. And I had to read it. At least I could have my tablet read it for me. Reading was hard. Sometimes the words jumped around or got all mixed up.

I didn't have enough time to watch a video before we would be thrusting enough for me to use the head. So I started looking at other stuff.

One of my favorite sites was *Science for Cubs, Kits, Kids, and Kittens.* I didn't even care that it listed 'kits' second when most folks knew that more species had kits than had cubs. It took science articles from a grown-up science magazine and made them more readable for younger creatures. Mommy liked it, too, because it didn't just include what she called 'fun science,' but talked about even pretty boring things, or things that a lot of children might think were boring.

The third article in the second issue that had been downloaded to my tablet while we were on Mars made my tail start wagging. "Breakthrough in True Artificial Gravity." As I had the tablet read it to me, it mentioned a lab in the belt on Ceres that had successfully tested a machine that would generate "tiny gravitational wells across a flat surface." It even mentioned that the biggest applications would be for space-going ships and habitats.

The idea that in the future, we might never have to go to zero-g was magical. Not only would that mean that I wouldn't have to deal with my zero-g tummy or the zero-g toilet. But Mommy and Daddy might not have to spend half the year on Earth so that Benji, Krissy, and I could grow up right. If we were in Earth's gravity all the time…

But, that would have to be expensive… And Daddy and Mommy were always worried about money. Sometimes Mommy worried that we might have to just live on Earth, where we could live in our house and have food and clothing, and everything we need—except for space and a lot of the nice things that having a ship means.

But a kit can dream.

———

Regina sat strapped into the main engineering seat across from Lauryn. "How does the reactor look?"

"We're at 100%, ready for throttle up."

She keyed the comms. "Bridge, engineering is ready for thrust."

"Roger engineering... go to 0.8g in 5...4...3...2...1...MARK!"

Her paw had already been on the lever before Jason reached one, so on "MARK," she started sliding it up, keeping her eyes on the thrust gauge. She had done this enough times; she could feel 0.8g within almost a hundredth of a g, but she still needed to watch the gauge because even the tiniest deviation in their thrust could mean missing Earth by tens of thousands of kilometers.

Regina had studied navigation math and orbital mechanics. She understood it well enough to help Benji through his current assignments, but she wasn't anywhere near as skilled at making the calculations as either Jason or Mark, both of whom could almost plot their launch vectors in their heads. Launching for a six to twelve-week journey between the planets, thrusting between 0.6g and 0.9g required aiming not at where your target was, but close to where it was going to be. But even then, there were adjustments needed to account for the slight curvature of space around the bodies' gravity wells and other factors that made things even more complicated.

In less than a second, the engines were set to 0.80g, the target thrust for their return to Earth. Regina locked the throttle at that position and confirmed that the control computer would maintain that thrust even through any variations in the flow or condition of the helium reaction mass. This wasn't the earliest crewed rockets that the humans flew (or might have flown—the exact history as to how automated they were was a bit murky), where the throttles were fully manual, nor even the first fusion rockets, which often expected a consistent output of pure helium from the fusion reactors. Sophisticated sensors would monitor the production of the reactor and make adjustments to the amount of helium being sent to the engines to account for the trace amounts of both hydrogen and lithium mixed into the helium, the temperature, and other factors to maintain the thrust within a fraction of a percent of where she'd set that throttle—and it would do so for weeks. The only thing the engineering crew would need to do over the next six weeks is ensure the reactor continues to operate at 100% and that hydrogen fuel is fed into it properly. And that could mostly be done via tablet and alert.

"Lauryn, Henley, how are things looking from your consoles?"

"My board is all green," Lauryn reported.

"Same down here," her brother chirped from the lower level.

"I'm going topside—well, to the galley." Regina started unbuckling her restraints. "It is time for this chief engineer to resume her other jobs, mother and galley officer."

She stood, feeling a million newtons heavier. She'd only been at Martian gravity, 0.38g, for a little over a week, with a few days at zero-g on either side. But being back at 0.8g was getting more noticeable every time. She knew that when they got back to Earth in six weeks, the full g would feel even heavier for a few days.

After a good shake to get used to the heavier gravity, she worked her way over to the ladder and climbed up. The rec deck was quiet. The kits were all in their dens. They usually were when they departed. All three of her children seemed to think that schoolwork was something to get out of the way as quickly as possible—at least for the first week or so of the trip. Then Benji, at least, would stop working on it unless pressed, leaving something, usually either his math or history, until the last minute.

She climbed the ladder to the lower berthing level and stopped to rest. Maybe she needed to do more exercise next time she's on Mars. She hoped it was that. Danny was eight. The last time she was this tired coming back to full thrust after a layover was more than eight years ago. She and Jace had a couple of good nights during this trip, and one on Mars. But she was too old now, wasn't she? And more than eight years when the first three had come within four years? No, this was just age, and maybe the first signs of Spacers, catching up with her.

At least she could hear the older kits in their dens. Benji sounded like he was recording a message for one of his... oh dear, he had a girl... no boyfriend. He was barely thirteen, and that message sounded a bit intimate. Nothing sexual, at least. But she'd better have Jace give him the talk before he started to get interested in that.

She then headed up one more level to the galley. A bit over a week earlier, she'd spent two hours securing it for its time in zero-g. Now she had to get it back for three weeks under thrust when it could be used like a normal, if small, kitchen. That meant unpacking the dishes and pans from the lockers and putting them back on the shelves, putting flatware back in the drawers, setting up the spice rack the way she liked, and a number of other tasks.

She quickly started with all of this, which, like so many shipboard tasks, was so automatic that she could do it while thinking about other things.

She had sent a preliminary report to Marsgov Child Services, reporting that Max, last name unknown, was a human child, approximately eight years old, with a sheepdog governess, and was probably being spanked by both father and governess, which was contrary to UC Child Protection guidelines. She wondered if there was something more she could do.

And there was Danny's feeling that he and Max had been being watched when they were playing in the park that morning. She'd felt it too. Red foxes, as a small predator species, were also prey. Whatever factors had led to most mammals gaining sentience rapidly during the Cataclysm had left them with many of their instincts intact. She was sure it was that sense, the sense that prey species had of being hunted, that made both her and Danny uneasy when they were in the park.

Her brother-in-law had been nervous since his night out as well. She was tempted to head into the cargo bay now that it was pressurized for transport and look into some of those crates of machine parts that he'd negotiated for and see if there was anything hidden there. Mark's access to the gray markets could have pushed him back into the black markets.

He wasn't the one who had spent six long Martian months locked up in a Martian prison for running drugs. That had been Jason. He'd gotten off with a slap on the wrist because he was considered a kit at the time. She'd gotten away with it... because she'd been able to call in a favor from her father, one she was still paying back by making sure that all three kits were getting fleet-approved and monitored educations, knowing that one or more of them was probably going to get dragged into the fleet one of these days.

Once she got the kitchen in order, she pulled out her favorite bowl —the antique ceramic one that she'd dug out of that old house in Barrington, six or so klicks from where their Earthside house was. She remembered that day, shortly after she and Jason had purchased the house with the profits from their first run as a married couple, only a year after he'd been released from the Marsgov Rehab Brig. They had trekked up to the site where pre-cataclysm homes were being dug, and all sorts of useful antique household items could be had as long as one was willing to use a spade or claws to dig them up. They had come back with a truckload of bowls, jars, and dishes. Only a few were on the ship; the rest stayed on earth. But this bowl and the mason jar she had set on the counter both stayed with her wherever she went.

She set the bowl under the synthesizer's output nozzle and instructed it to fill it with most of the ingredients she'd need: flour, salt, and honey. It spent a few minutes cranking through, sourcing the various amino acids and other base chemicals needed to produce the proper mixture, then fusing them into the ingredients before dumping them into the bowl. She then added water, carefully scooped some of the sourdough mother into the mixture, and stirred it together with her paws. She put a cloth over it, set it on the counter in a spot she knew would keep it at the correct temperature, and let it rise.

Next, she synthesized more flour and sugar, then added them to the mother's jar, secured the cloth lid, and put it back on its shelf.

When she turned, Danny was standing there. One sniff told her exactly why he'd come down from his den.

"Mommy, can I take a bath?"

"Yes, honey. Why don't you do it right now instead of waiting until after supper? Supper won't be for an hour or more. I'll let you use 450 millimeters today."

She knew that 450 millimeters was a bit generous, even though the water would be fully recycled, even that which evaporated and condensed elsewhere in the ship would eventually find its way back to the water recycling system. But they had a full tank, and it wasn't Danny she had to worry about. Benji had recently switched to showers, and he was taking as long as 5 minutes on some days. And she didn't buy his argument that the shampoo wasn't rinsing. She knew exactly how well the shampoo they stocked on the ship rinsed in the nearly distilled water from the showerhead.

She looked at the ceiling. "Jason, you were the one who insisted that we have kits."

CHAPTER 7

CHAPTER 7

Five days out from Mars, I was up on the bridge with Uncle Mark.

Daddy and Mommy were down in their berth, taking a nap. Mommy had been napping a lot on this trip, and I was worried she might be sick or something. Daddy had even fixed breakfast two mornings because Mommy wasn't feeling like cooking. I didn't like it when Daddy made breakfast. He had the synthesizer make cooked eggs. Mommy had it make eggs raw and then cooked them on the stove. And he had it make bread and toast it. I liked Mommy's bread better.

I was sitting in the sensor chair—we weren't at zero-g, so I wasn't strapped in, since I wouldn't float away. I had the helmet on. It was still too big, but that was OK. I was outside, or like I was the ship. And I loved that.

The tiny particles—micrometers—were flying by, tickling my whiskers. Some of the really big ones were being zapped by our ship's grid, a bunch of lasers that could automatically hit them and make them smaller so they wouldn't hurt us. But most of them were too small to hurt the ship.

I turned to look behind us. There was something… It looked like another ship was following us. It was tiny. I could make it bigger, but the image got fuzzy.

"Uncle Mark, someone is following us."

"Danny, that is just another ship from Mars to Earth that left shortly after us. They look like they are following."

I watched it for a few more minutes. I'd seen other ships before. They never looked quite like that. This one was in the wrong place… I can't explain it. But if they left just after us, they'd be off to the side differently. Maybe it's because I'm what Uncle Mark calls a "Born Spacer."

It looked to me like this ship was getting bigger. That was wrong. A ship getting bigger was moving faster. I'd done Benji's navigation math homework for him. If the ship was moving faster than us, thrusting at higher gs, it would miss Earth. That wasn't right.

I kept quiet for as long as I could, watching that other ship, until I was sure that it was getting bigger, moving faster, thrusting at higher gs. It took me a long time, maybe as much as an hour.

I must have been really still, because Uncle Mark tapped me on the shoulder. "Did you fall asleep again, Danno?"

"No, I've been watching that ship. It's getting bigger."

"Let me see."

I pulled the helmet off, and Uncle Mark slipped it on. I leaned over and started watching the pilot gauges. They didn't have to be watched all the time, but if someone was on the bridge, they were supposed to watch them. I only knew what a few of them meant, and all of them were where they should be.

Mark's shoulders sank, but other than that, he didn't say anything to me other than, "Danny, isn't it about time for you to go get supper?"

Three days later, I was in my den when an alarm went off that I'd never heard. I was supposed to be asleep, but I'd been watching one of the old medical dramas, or what I thought was supposed to be a medical drama, when I first started watching it. It was called *Doctor Who,* but it wasn't about a doctor at all, just a human, except he wasn't a human, who called himself "Doctor" and traveled in time and space and got into all sorts of strange adventures with a bunch of humans. It was weird, silly, and really scary at times. And it had lots of episodes.

I climbed out of my den and went down toward the rec deck, where I thought everyone else was, to see what was going on.

When I got there, things were weird. Mommy and Daddy were looking at each other, as confused as I was. Benji and Krissy were sitting in the corner, looking scared. They were all looking toward the airlock. But why would anyone be looking at the airlock when we were thrusting? Nobody would go out of the ship at thrust. An EVA at thrust was someone that was only done under the most dire of an emergency—and if it were that bad, Daddy would have all of us in our suits first.

I ran over to stand next to Benji and Krissy. I figured that was where I should be.

Ramon dropped down the ladder. He didn't climb down; he jumped from the lower habitat level, where he had his berth, and landed. He had a gun in one paw and another in a holster over one shoulder and around his waist. That was scary, but what was scarier was the look in the ferret's eyes.

Then Uncle Mark came down the ladder. He was even scarier. His ears were flat, his tail was bushed out, and he had a darter—a dart gun —in his paw. He turned and fired at Ramon. The ferret fell to the deck. He then turned and looked right at me. He mouthed something that looked like it might have been "Sorry, Danny."

Suddenly, I felt something sharp hit my shoulder. Then there was a burning where it hit. My eyes grew heavy and… blackness.

————

After Mark chased Danny off the bridge, he pulled the sensor helmet back on and loaded the bootleg enhancements that he'd installed shortly after they started thrusting into the suite. As soon as they processed the information, he had a better view of the ship that was coming their way. It was still too far to get a clear visual, but the long-range painted a picture that confirmed his fears—maybe not his worst.

He knew that there were only a few ships that could safely make the kind of thrust needed to chase and match a small freighter thrusting at 0.8g, and what he saw confirmed that this was one. He was looking at a UC Fleet fast frigate.

If the UC was after them, it wasn't for forged tax stamps on whiskey bottles. They'd slap them with the duties when they reached Earth, along with the fine, which would wipe out any profit they'd have made on the whiskey. No, this was about whatever XHum000 and her partners had all but forced Mark to carry.

There was one reality about running freight between planets within a system: you couldn't run and hide. There weren't enough rocks in the Solar System to hide on, and they were too far apart.

He pulled up his tablet and fed it the sensor data before purging the logs of information about the pursuing ship. He had three days to get ready—three days to figure out how to save as many of the creatures on this ship from the mistake he'd made to save Danny from what might have been a purely made-up threat.

He wanted to keep the threat from Jason and Regina. He had already determined that Regina was pregnant. Not only had she been sick the last two mornings, but her odor had already started to shift subtly. He really hated that shift, because it made her more attractive to him. He'd never stopped loving her, at least a bit. She'd been happily married to his brother for fifteen years, and he'd long accepted that. But part of him still wished that he'd been the Bartlett brother she'd fallen for.

That was a foolish desire. He'd been a kit when they met Regina Schroder, rebellious daughter of UC Fleet Captain Kingsley Schroder and a dropout from the UC Academy. There was no real way she was going to fall from the teenage kit when the handsome and, more or less, fully grown, older Jason Bartlett had been there to charm her. Their run-in with Marsgov law enforcement, and Jason's six months in the brig for the drug running all three of them had been equally guilty of, had only made him that much more attractive in her eyes. And after that, Mark had been relegated permanently to brother-in-law and kit's uncle territory.

And, now, he'd gone and mistaken his duty as uncle to the kit that was most like him, and put the entire family in danger of something. Probably getting caught by the UC Fleet was better than the alternatives, but what would it mean?

At this point, Regina's father probably wouldn't be able to get her off. If she and Jason were arrested, they could all do time, and he had no idea how long that could be because he had no idea what they were carrying. If that happened, the kits might end up with either his father —who was dying and might not see the year out—or with Regina's father, who they didn't even know. Or they might end up in Earthgov or Marscgov foster care, and that could be worse.

Over the next two days, Mark kept an eye on the approaching ship and the rest of the crew. He was able to confirm that it was the UC fast frigate Sparrow. He kept it off the sensor logs, which meant that he was the only one on the ship who knew they would be boarded as soon as the frigate could reach them and match speed.

He started formalizing a plan. He needed to keep as many of the crew safe. To do that, he'd have to make a sacrifice. He'd sacrifice the one thing he could—which was more than he wanted to, perhaps much more than he could afford. But it was the only way.

When the boarding alarm went off, Mark was ready. He'd been in his berth since it was evening shift, and everything was on automation.

He grabbed his darter and confirmed that it was loaded with light sublethal. The darts would knock out anyone on the ship, but wouldn't do any long-lasting damage, even to the baby that Regina was carrying. But he'd only shoot the one or two creatures he was most worried about, either hurting the fleeters or seeing his downfall.

He stepped out of his bunk to see Ramon jumping down to the rec deck. That had been one of his concerns. When the ferret had joined the crew, Mark had looked into his UC Fleet record a bit. He couldn't get into the sealed records related to his less-than-honorable discharge, but his service record was clear. He'd served on UC Nightingale, which had cleaned up more than its share of pirate attacks. He was sure that the ferret believed that there were pirates on the other side of the lock. He'd seen the ferret's slug throwers. The ferret was going to kill someone—either the UC fleeters coming through the lock, or the family he didn't want to fall into the hands of the pirates, maybe both.

Mark followed as quickly as his footpaws could, landing on the floor of the rec deck only seconds after the ferret.

Ramon was on full alert.

Mark only had seconds to take him out before he became the ferret's first target. He flipped off the safety on the darter and pressed its trigger, and heard the sound of the compressed air as the dart flew, hitting the ferret right in his bare chest, just above the leather of the holster for his second gun.

Ramon swayed for half a second before collapsing to the deck.

Mark then turned to survey the room. All three kits were grouped. Good, he had a chance to keep any of them from seeing him get arrested. Danny was standing, and he was the most important of the three to spare. He mouthed an apology, then shot, catching the youngest of Jason and Regina's children in the shoulder.

He shifted to fire at Benji, but his brother hit his right arm, knocking the darter from his paw.

Things went into slow motion at that moment.

The UC Fleet overrode the airlock code, and it opened. A dozen heavily armed fleeters stormed in.

Mark held his paws up. "I'm the one you want. Jason and Regina knew nothing about it. I made the deal for whatever is hidden in the machine parts."

Two of the fleeters tackled him to the deck, pulling his arms quickly behind his back and sliding the cuffs around his wrists tightly. He was then pulled to his feet and dragged off the ship and onto the Sparrow.

———

I woke up feeling really icky. I was lying on a cot in the galley. Daddy had a cold cloth on my head.

Henley, one of the cavies Mommy hired to help in engineering, was sitting doing the same to Ramon.

It took me a bit to remember why I was feeling icky, and why my shoulder stung like my paw had when I got too close to a hornet's nest when we were Earthside when I was six.

"Daddy, why did Uncle Mark shoot me?"

"He didn't want you to see him get arrested?"

"Uncle Mark did something bad?"

"He had us carrying really bad stuff for some really bad creatures who wanted to hurt a lot of creatures on Earth because they don't like something."

"Can you believe humanists using foxes to carry their explosives?" Henley commented.

"Daddy, what is a humanist?"

Daddy leaned over. "A humanist is a human who thinks that they should be in charge because they became sentient first. And they do bad things because of it."

"And they made Uncle Mark put bad stuff on our ship?"

"Yes."

"And the UC arrested him for it?"

"Yes, and he might go to jail for a long time. We won't know until we get to Earth what happened to him."

I started to cry. "So Uncle Mark isn't on the ship anymore?"

"No, kitto. Uncle Mark got taken away. But he made sure he was the only one taken away. And the UC Fleeters took away all the bad stuff. We're safe. We could have blown up if something had gone wrong."

"Why isn't Mommy helping me, or Ramon?"

"Mommy had an… Mommy was going to have another kit, but it wasn't healthy. She had what is called a miscarriage. She's in with Lauryn in our berth, recovering."

"So, who is watching the ship?"

"Benji and Krissy are doing what they can until you are well enough to go up to your den. Do you feel good enough to sleep in your den for a while?"

"Yes, Daddy. Then I can help you watch the bridge until we get home to Earth."

"I'll let you and Benji help as much as I need. Since I don't have my co-pilot, I'll need my three kits to step up."

My tail started wagging. "I'll do what I can, Daddy. But I'm only eight."

"I know, Danno. But you are a natural born spacer—even if you get a bit space sick in zero-g like your father, and hate the zero-g toilet like both your parents."

"You don't like the zero-g toilet?"

"It… it really hurts my privates. I've read that they have nearly perfected artificial gravity. If I can get a loan, or if the UC Fleet doesn't confiscate all of the money that Mark got paid, maybe I'll see if we can get some put on our ship as soon as it's available for small cargo boats."

ABOUT THE AUTHOR

Randall Fox is the pseudonym Ron Oakes uses when writing novellas about Randall and his friends.

Ron Oakes is a computer scientist, science fiction and fantasy fan, and self-published fantasy writer based in Albuquerque, New Mexico. Some of his earliest memories include watching *Star Trek* on weekday afternoons and desiring to work on computers like those found on the U.S.S. Enterprise. Not long afterward, he saw *Star Wars* in its original incarnation (before it became *Episode IV: A New Hope*).

In the late 1970s, through his Boy Scouts troop, he was introduced to Dungeons & Dragons. At around the same time, he was introduced to the *Chronicles of Prydain* by Lloyd Alexander. These combined to create a love of fantasy.

After college, he moved to the Chicago Suburbs. His love of D&D and other tabletop role-playing games led him to discover organized Science Fiction Fandom in the early 1990s. As a fan and convention runner, he has worked on and run conventions in Chicago, San Diego, and Albuquerque.

He is married to another fan and works as a government contractor in Albuquerque. He shares his house with his wife, four cats, over 300 robots, multiple lightsabers, more artwork than the walls can hold, several dragons, and assorted stuffed animals—not all of which are from this world.

ALSO BY RANDALL FOX

UNITED CREATURES UNIVERE STORIES

Half-Tonne of Silence

Trial and Consequences

Danny and his Grandfathers

RANDALL FOX STORIES

Flight of the Heretics

The Prey's Rebellion

The Wolf and The Parliament

The Hermitage and The Henge

The Tunnel and The Ox

The Duchess and The Fox

The Cougar and The Quest

The Books and The Guardian

The Kitsune and The Kit

The Transformation and The Future

The Pup and The Adventure

The Moose and The Crown

The Stoat and The Pilgrims

The Muzzle and The Pursuit

The Potion and The Madness

The Priest and The Gang

The Lord and The Fires

The Wolf and The Champion

The Bear and The Squirrel

The Reindeer and the Stone Circle

The Catacombs and The Wolf

The Friends and The Walk

The Trickster and The Cabin

The Fox and The Letter

The Mouse and The Squirrels

The Executor and The Revenge

INSPECTOR BEAUREGARD STORIES

The Inspector and The Robber

The Inspector and The Magistrate

The Inspector And His Son

The Advocate and The Duke

———

AS RON OAKES

The Phoenix Knives

9 781971 636016